Truesilver

Truesilver

Book Four
The Last Werewolf Hunter

by

William Woodall

Jeremiah Press · *Antoine, Arkansas*

Jeremiah Press
PO Box 3
Antoine, AR 71922

Cover image by Dan Eckert and William Woodall.

First published by Jeremiah Press on 06/12/2013.

Printed in the United States of America.

This book is printed on acid-free paper.

ISBN 978-0-9819641-6-4

For all the fans,

Who asked for this book.

With the Lord one day is as a thousand years,
And a thousand years as one day.
-2 Peter 3:8

Thoughts of a Werewolf Hunter
By Zachary James Trewick

"Not all the monsters in the world are cursed ones."

"Beauty is still beautiful, no matter what the circumstances."

"Love is a beautiful thing, and the whole world bows down in awe at the sight of it, they say."

"It's better to go down fighting for what's right and true, than to live forever as a hypocrite. I knew that. I've always known it, in the way that all men have known it since the beginning of time. Mors ante infamium; death before dishonor. The battle cry of everyone from the legions of Rome to the street gangs of Houston. Everyone knows the truth of it."

"I had sworn an oath to God Himself to fight evil to the utmost of my power; not to make deals with it."

"There are people like that; toadies and wannabes who are too feeble and dimwitted to accomplish anything themselves, but they love to participate vicariously through what other people do. All bullies have their hangers-on. All tormenters have their suck-ups and tale-bearers. The heart is just as black either way."

"Magic and miracles are not the same thing at all. A magician wants power and thinks he can bend the world to his own will whenever and however he pleases, good or bad. Miracles are always a gift, and they're given when God chooses, never when we do."

"You never really learn how much you love a place till you start thinking about leaving it behind, and then you have a tendency to pull it close to your heart while you still can."

"It's perfectly all right to pray about things which took place in the past, as long as you don't know what the outcome was. God is outside of time completely, and therefore so are your prayers to Him. In that way, it's quite possible for you to be the partial cause of something that happened long before you were even born."

Contents

Chapter One

I thought we were done with curses and wolves. I'd had more than enough spookiness like that to satisfy me for a lifetime.

It was the first of summer, right after we got out of school, and the long days stretched ahead of us full of freedom and promise. Me and Cam had a job baling hay and building fences for old man Barling on his cattle ranch, and we were playing Dixie League baseball with a good chance of making it to the world series later in the year if all went well. Our only real chores were to groom the horses and sometimes to baby sit Josiah while Justin and Eileen were at work, but those things were easy.

In other words, we had nothing to look forward to except good times and fun for the next three months.

Or so I thought.

When Jolie asked us to come down to Natchitoches to help wake up all those sleeping people in the store room, it didn't seem like such a big deal at first. Just an extra pair of hands in case somebody woke up rowdy, you know. I was cool with that.

So we drove down there early one Friday afternoon to get started on the project, and the house was quiet when we got there. John and Sarah Doucet were out of town for the weekend, on a mini-trip to Cancun from what I heard. Lifestyles of the rich and famous, I guess.

The store room was every bit as dusty and dank as I remembered, with the same old shelves of bottles filled with dust, and the same rough wooden table under an incongruously fancy chandelier. It was me and Cameron, Jolie, and her cousin Matthieu. He's nineteen years old and sort of reminds me of a street thug, honestly. He's got the dark brown hair and eyes that Cajuns often have, with a sparse little goatee and some serious muscle. Definitely not the kind of dude you'd want to meet in a dark alley late at night, even though I'm sure he'd laugh if I ever told him that. He's really one of the nicest people you'd ever want to know; he just doesn't look like it.

"So, what do y'all think? Who's first?" Matthieu said out loud, rubbing his hands together while we all stood and stared at the dusty bottles.

"Just grab one, Zach," Jolie finally told me, since I was the one standing closest to the shelf. I shrugged and picked a bottle at random; there was really no way to be scientific about it.

"What about this one?" I asked. It looked just like all the others, and all it said on the label was *Joan Rusk, December 23, 1864.*

"All right. Hold on a sec, and I'll see if I can find her. Then we'll decide if she's a good pick," Matthieu said. He went to the big metal cabinet against the back wall and started thumbing through files till he found the one we needed.

"Um. . . here it is. Joan Rusk. Two-member pod, operated out of Titus County, Texas, from 1863 to 1864. Nailed that one pretty fast, didn't we?" he remarked, reading from the file.

"Only two members?" I asked.

"Yeah, that's a little bit unusual, isn't it? But it looks like the ringleader was a young one; only seventeen years old when we caught her," he said.

"Still just a kid, then," I said.

"Apparently," he shrugged, still looking at the file.

"So what's it say? Is she good to go or not?" Jolie asked after a while.

"Hmm. . . could be. There's not much in here about her. The case worker didn't seem to have much trouble catching her, or the sister either. Not very rich. In fact it looks like she didn't own anything but a horse and the clothes on her back. Doesn't say if she attacked people or animals or what. Let's see if there's anything about the sister," he said, riffling through the pages.

"Okay, the sister's name is Annabelle; sixteen years old. Looks like she was never a wolf, though. Just got caught up in the crossfire, apparently," he said.

"So we've got her, too?" I asked.

"Supposed to. Can you grab her off the shelf, Zach? Might as well get them both done at the same time," he said. I looked, but I saw neither hide nor hair of a bottle with Annabelle Rusk on it.

"Well, dang it, she's not here," I said after a minute of searching the bottles.

"She probably got misplaced, that's all. I'm sure she's there," he said.

"So does that mean we go ahead and wake up this one anyway, or should we find a different one?" Cam asked.

"Oh, I guess she'll do. Let's go ahead," Matthieu said.

He emptied the bottle into that same old green ceramic ashtray that I'd used for Jason Golden last fall, and then poured a little bit of sweet water on top of it. He stirred up the muddy mixture with a pencil, and then it didn't take long before the old girl was laid out on the table, seemingly not much worse for the wear.

Jolie dressed her while the rest of us turned away; we hadn't known what size clothes she might need, so we'd done the best we could with some stretchy sweat pants and an extra large t-shirt. It wasn't the prettiest outfit in the world by a long shot, but we could always find her some better clothes later on.

"Okay, guys, she's decent," Jolie said from behind us, and we turned around. Cameron whistled, and I might have done the same thing if Jolie hadn't been standing right there. But it's kind of tasteless (not to mention dangerous) to do things like that in front of your girlfriend, so I bit my tongue and kept quiet.

"She's pretty," Cam said, pointing out the obvious. And so she was, in an old-fashioned kind of way. What I mean is, she looked like she'd never cut her hair a single day in her life, or plucked her eyebrows, or shaved her legs, or done any of those things girls nowadays like to do so they'll look nice. She had the kind of tan you get from spending a lot of time outside, but not the kind that comes from tanning beds or laying in the sun on purpose. She had some faint freckles across the bridge of her nose and her brown hair was flecked with gold here and there. She was also short; probably no more than five feet tall at the most. But nevertheless, she was nice looking.

"Yeah, I guess she's okay," Jolie agreed, brushing it aside. Cam pricked his thumb and smeared some blood on the girl's forehead, and that seemed to be enough. After a few seconds she breathed deeply and opened her eyes, which were green as spring leaves.

"Joan?" he asked, and she moaned.

"Where am I?" she finally replied. Not surprising; that's almost always the first thing you want to know when you wake up in a strange place.

"You're in Louisiana. There's been some trouble but we're here to help you," he told her.

"Who are you? What happened?" she asked, rubbing her eyes and looking around. I didn't think there was anything in the room which would have looked *too* peculiar to her 1864 eyes, but then again I'm not a trained historian, either. Evidently there wasn't, because she didn't say anything.

"My name's Cameron, and these are my friends. I'm afraid it'll take a little while to explain what happened and how you got here, but if you'll bear with us for a few minutes we'll tell you everything," he promised.

Joan didn't say much to that, and I noticed her eyes roving the room. There was an old letter-opener lying on top of the file cabinet, and as soon as I saw her gaze fix on it, I knew there was about to be trouble.

"Hey, she- " I started, but that was all I had time to say before the girl leaped off the table and snatched up that letter opener faster than you would think anybody could possibly move, especially somebody who just woke up from the dust sleep. I'd seen what *that* did to people, and I was amazed she could get up on her feet that fast. She was one tough cookie.

"Nobody come any closer!" she yelled, brandishing the letter opener like it was a dagger. Nobody moved an inch; somehow none of us doubted she was really good with a knife.

She was breathing hard and didn't look like she felt very well, but she wasn't letting that get in her way. She started edging towards the door, and we realized she meant to run if she could.

"Listen, Joan, you don't know what it's like out there. Things have changed. It's not like what you think it is. Please, let us help you," Jolie said.

"I'll help myself, thanks. Y'all just stay back," she said.

"Look, we don't mean you any harm, and we won't keep you from leaving if you really want to. But Jolie is right. It's a different world out there than anything you ever saw before, and it's dangerous, too. Go look and see, but then come back and let us help you," Matthieu told her.

"Why should I believe anything you say?" she demanded, jerking the letter-opener at us. She was still inching her way toward the door, and we were carefully backing away from her at the same time.

"You don't have to take our word for it. Go see for yourself that we're telling the truth, and remember we never tried to keep you from leaving. We'll help you if you'll let us," Matthieu repeated.

I thought I saw a flicker of doubt in her green eyes, but then again maybe not. However that might be, she made a sudden dash for the door and yanked it open, and then she was gone before any of us could say another word.

"Come on!" Matthieu yelled, and we all ran outside after her. What she thought about the flower garden I don't know, but it didn't take the girl five heartbeats to find the back gate and disappear into the alley behind Sarah Doucet's house.

"Great. We've let a lunatic loose on the world," Jolie hissed in frustration.

"Don't worry about it. Let her go," I said.

"We can't do that. She won't know *anything*. She might walk right out in front of a car and get killed," Matthieu said.

"Yeah, I know, but that's the thing. We told her we wouldn't stop her from leaving if she wanted to. So let her leave. Maybe she'll see that we meant what we said and then come back and let us help her," I explained.

"She didn't seem too keen on getting help from anybody, much less us," Cam pointed out.

"Yeah, but I bet she'll change her mind, though. Just wait a few minutes, till the first time she sees a car. She'll come back," I said.

"And what if she doesn't? What then?" Matthieu demanded.

"Well, in that case she'll just have to do the best she can. We can't help her if she won't let us. She looks like she's pretty good at taking care of herself when she needs to," I said.

"Yeah, that she does," Matthieu finally agreed with a sigh.

We all went to the patio to wait and see if Joan would come back. We had a pretty good view of the back gate from there, and it was better than going back inside the store room where she might not remember how to find us. After a while, Matthieu and

Jolie went inside to fetch some lemonade and sandwich materials from the kitchen, and me and Cameron stayed out on the patio to watch the gate.

"You really think she'll be back?" he asked in a low voice, and I shrugged.

"No way to tell. I *think* she will, but I guess you never know," I said.

"It's been almost thirty minutes," he pointed out.

"Yeah, but all we can do is wait and see," I said. There was a pause, and then he must have decided it was time to change the subject.

"She was a little spitfire, wasn't she?" he asked, grinning. It hadn't seemed very funny to me at the time, back there in the store room with her holding us off at knife-point (or letter-opener-point), but I guess it's amazing what you can laugh at in hindsight.

"Yeah, I guess she was, at that. But it takes all kinds to make a world, they say," I agreed, smiling a little bit myself.

Matt and Jolie got back with the lemonade and the cold cuts right about then, and for a while all of us were busy fixing our food. It seemed like a normal day, almost. But all of us kept glancing at the back gate while we ate, and whenever anybody tried to start up a conversation it always petered out before long. We ended up eating our sandwiches in silence. We waited most of the afternoon to see if she'd come back, but finally I had to confess that I'd been wrong about her.

"Guess she's not coming back after all," I finally admitted.

"Don't worry about it, Zach. Like you said, she'll just have to handle things on her own. We did the best we could," Matthieu sighed.

"I was so *sure* of it, though," I said.

"So what do we do, write that one off and try again? We've still got four or five hours worth of daylight left," Cameron asked.

"Yeah, let's do that. We can't let one setback stop us," Matthieu agreed, and we adjourned to the store room and got ready to start over.

"Maybe we should pick somebody from not so long ago, this time. They might not freak out quite so much," Jolie suggested.

I was closest to the shelf again this time, so I carefully picked up one of the bottles closest to the end.

"What about this one? Andrew Garza. Not even two years ago," I said, holding up the bottle for them to see. Then I noticed that Jolie had turned ashen-faced.

"What's wrong?" I asked.

"No, Zach. We're never waking *them* up. That's the New Mexico pod," she said, like she expected me to instantly recognize the significance of that. I did vaguely remember her mentioning a particularly evil pod in New Mexico, but she'd never told me any details.

"What's so bad about them?" I asked.

"That was one of the worst pods we ever had to fight. They almost killed Matthieu before we finally nailed them," she said.

"Well. . . yeah, but the Curse is gone now. It shouldn't matter anymore at this point, should it?" I asked, confused.

"There are a lot of people in the world who don't need a werewolf curse to make them do awful things. For them, that's just icing on the cake," she said.

"What do you mean?" I asked.

"There were four members of that pod, three brothers and a sister, and they used to kill people they caught on the highways out there, all over southern New Mexico and west Texas. It went on for years before we caught them. The Garzas were more than just wolves, though; they were sorcerers, too, and Andrew Garza was even a pretty intelligent scientist, I might add. He was the ringleader," she said.

She went on to tell us more than I cared to know about the Garza pod. Sometimes there are things that feel like they put a weight on your soul that will never go away however long you live. The stuff the Garzas did was like that, and I'm not going to darken anybody else's heart by repeating what I heard that night. It's enough to say that I understood completely what it was that made her face turn white when I first mentioned them.

Not all the monsters in the world are cursed ones, that's for sure.

Dr. Garza (that was Andrew) apparently had his finger in a lot of different pies. He was a physicist at the White Sands Missile Range and a professor at New Mexico State University in Las Cruces, among other things. He and his brother's sorcery ran toward the destructive side; fire and lightning and explosions. Not to mention curses and speaking to the dead and some really bad stuff like that. It reminded me of the things Daniel Trewick used to talk about in his journal, only ten times worse. The Garzas were no amateurs, and the worst thing of all was that they were necromancers.

That is, they could take dead people and turn them into zombies who would do whatever they told them to do. That's one reason they killed all those people, since apparently the bodies had to be fresh and they needed to kill them slowly.

See what I mean about not wanting to know?

I don't think I would ever in a million years have imagined a professional scientist who also practiced magic on the side; the two things seemed like such glaring opposites.

"That's a strange combination to be involved in," I said.

"It might seem that way at first, but not really when you think about it. Dr. Garza was all about power. He'd do anything he had to do to get it. Science, magic, curses. . . all those things were just means to an end, as far as he was concerned," she said.

"Means to what end?" I asked.

"The ability to hurt people and get away with it. He enjoyed watching people suffer, Zach, in every possible way you can imagine. All four of them were like that, even though he was by far the worst. In fact we never *did* catch the sister. If the Garzas got out, I don't know what they might do. Is that enough? Don't ask me any more!" she said.

"All right, then. Why don't you put his bottle in the file cabinet, so nobody grabs it again by mistake," I suggested.

"Good idea. Grab Gabe and Orem, too; that's his brothers," Matthieu said. Those two turned out to be easy to find, and soon they were all safely stashed away in the bottom of the file cabinet. Then I picked through the bottles again till I found another recent possibility.

"What about Ashley Dolan?" I asked.

"Hmm. . . I don't remember her. Let me look real quick," Matthieu said, and after a few minutes of rummaging through the files he pulled out another manila folder.

"Okay, here she is. Ashley Dolan, four member pod out of Sarasota, Florida, brought in three years ago. Looks like it was Ashley, her husband Henry, and their two daughters, Daisy and Suzanne. She's a nurse, he's an optician, and the girls are still in high school. Notes only mention hunting cattle. They ought to be all right," he said, scanning over the information.

"Sounds like a dull bunch of wolves, if you ask me," Cameron muttered.

"Yeah, well, dull is good right now," Matthieu reminded him.

I fetched the other three Dolans from the shelf, and set them on the table.

"Do you think we want them knowing about this place? Maybe we should take them somewhere else first, before we wake them up," I suggested. I hadn't thought of that idea with Joan, but it was better late than never.

"Nah, I'm not too worried about it. Nobody would believe them anyway, even if they said something. Besides that, we'll have to take them all the way to Shreveport to get them a plane ticket home, and we can blindfold them till then. That way they won't actually know where we are, and needless to say we won't give them our real names. I doubt they'll object to any of that; they've got good reasons to be grateful to us for waking them up," Matthieu said.

"Yeah, I guess," I replied, thinking to myself that gratitude can be an awfully unreliable thing to depend on.

So we woke them up, one at a time, and dressed them and fed them and explained things to them, as best we could. And you know, in that particular case, Matthieu was right. They were too grateful to be alive again to ask too many questions. He bought all of them a plane ticket back to Florida, and then we had to drive them to the airport in Shreveport.

That took several hours, and by the time we saw them off and made it back to Natchitoches, it was way past dark.

"Why don't y'all just stay here tonight? There's no reason to drive all that way back to Texarkana tonight," Matthieu suggested.

"Sure, why not?" Cam said, answering for both of us. We were both supposed to go to work for Jeb Barling the next afternoon, but that still left plenty of time to get back as long as we didn't stay too late in the morning.

So that's what we did. The Doucets had plenty of room in that big house for ten people to spend the night if they'd wanted, but with all of us there and Matthieu's parents out of town it reminded me of an oversized slumber party. We sat on the patio for a while after we got back, I guess still vainly hoping that Joan might show up.

"Well, at least one of them went pretty well," I said.

"Yeah, I guess so. I think the Dolans will be all right, once they settle down. But I think in the future you might have a point about not waking them up in the store room, though. It might be better to take them somewhere close to wherever they live, and then do it there," Matthieu said, and I nodded.

"We can think about it tomorrow," I told him.

"Which reminds me, I better go lock the store room before everybody goes to bed. Don't want anybody snooping around in there after everybody's asleep," Matthieu said.

"You mean Joan?" I guessed.

"Well, yeah, among others. I don't *think* she'll be back, and even if she does there's probably not much harm she can do, but I'll still feel better with it locked," he explained.

"I wonder where she ended up. She's got a hard life ahead of her, all alone like that," I said. I wasn't especially interested in Joan anymore, honestly; I'm not too fond of people who pull knives on me when I'm trying to help them. Not even beautiful 150 year old girls. But I did feel sorry for her a little bit.

"No telling," Jolie shrugged.

We all walked out there with Matthieu, and it was already pitch black inside the tunnel when we pushed the vines aside.

"Hold on a sec," he said, pulling a mini-flashlight out of his pocket. I was about to say something funny about how he was always prepared for anything, but then he clicked on the light and we all gasped.

The door was standing wide open.

Chapter Two

"This is *not* good," Matthieu said, and I couldn't have agreed more. He might not have locked the door when we left, but I knew darned well he'd shut it.

"Uh. . . you don't think Rob or Celine-" Cameron began, and Matthieu cut him off with a brisk shake of his head.

"I doubt they'd come over here, and even if they did, there's no way they'd leave the door open like that. In fact, they'd probably jump all over me for being careless and leaving it unlocked even while we went to Shreveport. They're real strict about things like that. But come on, let's go see what's up," he said, heading straight for the door.

One thing I have to say about Matthieu; he's fearless. Sometimes a little too much so, for my taste. I grabbed his arm and held him back.

"Hold on a second. Let's grab something to fight with, just in case we need to," I said. There wasn't much to be had, but we all grabbed sharp sticks from the garden. Better than nothing.

Armed with those, we slowly crept closer till we reached the door. Matthieu cautiously flipped the light switch on, and we all sighed with relief when we saw that the room was empty.

"Nothing here," I said, lowering my toad-sticker. Then I noticed an anomaly. We'd left the Dolans' bottles sitting on the table, along with the half-empty jug of sweet water. Now there were *seven* empty bottles, not four, and the water jug was dry as a bone.

My throat went dry, and I swallowed hard before I could speak.

"See that?" I whispered, nudging Matthieu's arm and pointing at the table.

"Come on. Let's find out who they are," he said, surprisingly calmly. I got to the table first and picked up the first bottle I could reach.

"Orem Garza," I said, reading the label aloud. My heart almost stopped in my chest, and even Matthieu's face went pale. He quickly snatched the other two bottles from the table.

"Gabe and Andrew. But *how?*" he hissed, setting the bottles back down. I would have loved an answer to that question, myself.

"Come on, let's go," Matthieu said, almost as soon as he put the bottles down.

"Go where?" I asked.

"Back in the house. It might not be safe out here with *him* loose again," he said.

I didn't say a word while he locked the door and marched straight across the garden to the back door. As soon as we were all inside, he set the alarm system immediately.

"It was Joan; it had to be," Jolie said immediately.

"But that doesn't make any sense. How would *she* know what to do, and why *them?*" I objected.

"Those are some really great questions, Zach. I'd love to find out what the answers are. But in the meantime, I think Jolie is right; who else could it have been? It was nobody in this house, and it wasn't my parents or Aunt Angie or Rob or Celine. Marc is still in France, and nobody else even knows about the store room. It *had* to be her," Matthieu said.

"But *how?*" Cameron asked.

"I bet she came back while we were busy with the Dolans. If she was quiet enough she could have heard us talking in there and figured out what to do," I suggested. It seemed unlikely that she could have been that stealthy, but it was the only idea I could think of that made any sense at all.

"Yeah, but that still doesn't explain the why part. Why would she want to wake up one of the sleepers anyway, much less one of *them?*" Jolie objected.

All I could do was shrug at that; I didn't have a clue.

"That's not important right now. The only thing that matters is that they're loose, and if she's the one that woke them up then it won't be long before she's a dead girl. Plain and simple. They won't thank her for helping them," Matthieu said. All of us were silent at that.

"So what do we do?" I asked, and the question kind of hung there in air, unanswered. The Garzas might not be werewolves anymore, but they still had their sorcery and Andrew at least still had his brilliant mind. Those things were more than enough to make them very dangerous enemies. But on the other hand, we couldn't let them escape, either.

"Come on," Matthieu said decisively, leaving the kitchen.

"What are we doing?" I asked.

"Just wait; you'll see," he said, and we all followed him to a locked room in the center of the house. It looked like an office inside, but as soon as he opened the door he immediately went to the back wall and tapped out a code with his fingers, in a spot which didn't appear to be anything but bare wallpaper. But as soon as he finished, a panel popped open that you never would've guessed was there.

Inside was a rack of pistols and a shotgun, all of them polished and ready to use at a moment's notice. Matthieu grabbed one of the pistols for each of us, expertly checking to make sure they were loaded before handing them out. He acted like he'd been born with a gun in his hand, he was so casual about it.

As for me, yeah, I'm a pretty good shot with a rifle, but I've never had much call to use a pistol before. It felt heavy and lethal in my hand, and I hoped it didn't show how unfamiliar I was with it.

I noticed that it was loaded with silver bullets; a leftover from the werewolf days, no doubt. But that was okay. It's not like regular humans are immune to silver bullets or anything.

"What are we doing?" I asked again.

"We've got to find them before they get too far away. I know Andrew too well; he was my case to start with. The first thing he'll do is run as far from Natchitoches as he thinks he's got time for, and then he'll go to ground someplace where he can lay hid for a while. If he does that we'll never find him, and then you can kiss Joan goodbye. He *might* keep her alive till then, if he thinks she's useful as a bargaining chip or maybe as a distraction to throw us off his trail. But once he finds a good hiding place he won't need her for those things anymore. She'll be more trouble than she's worth at that point, and then he'll write her off without a blink. Mark my words," Matthieu said coolly.

"And she had to pick *that* one to wake up," I muttered.

"Maybe that's not so surprising, you know. She didn't seem to like us much, if you remember," Cameron said.

"What difference would that make?" Jolie asked.

"Well, I don't know. Now that I think about it, maybe she got scared after she saw all this freaky modern stuff, and she thought we were the ones who brought her here, and she overheard us talking about the Garzas. Maybe she figured anybody who was an enemy of ours must be a friend of hers," he said. Matt frowned, but he must have been thinking it over seriously, at least.

"That's a lot of maybes, Cam," he finally said.

"True, but we can't do anything right now but guess, anyway," Cam said.

"Which is the most sensible thing I've heard anybody say all evening. We're wasting time trying to guess what Joan was thinking. We need to figure out what to do right this minute, or pretty soon there'll be nothing we *can* do," Jolie said flatly.

"Not so fast. It'll be dangerous without the rings. We'll have to be careful and stay hid for as long as we can and then hit them fast and hard," Matthieu said. Nobody questioned that; when it came to tactics he was an expert, and we all respected him.

"So what do we do, then?" I asked.

"First let's try to figure out where they went and how long it's been. We left here with the Dolans about five o'clock, so we have to assume she woke up the Garzas not much later than that, if we're right about the whole idea of her overhearing us. It wouldn't make sense for her to hang around twiddling her thumbs," he went on.

"Makes sense. Okay, let's say they left here about five thirty. The first thing they'd have to do would be to find some clothes. They couldn't walk through town naked for very long without attracting attention," Jolie said.

"They'd have to break into somebody's house for that, and I bet I know exactly which one, too," Matthieu said.

"Which one?" I asked.

"The Tolberts. They're right across the alley from our place, and they're out of town for three weeks. That would have been the perfect place for them to hit," he said.

"Do they have an alarm system?" Cameron asked.

"I don't know, but it's still my best guess. We better go over there and check it out. Andrew's smart, though; he may have set up a diversion to waste our time, or even a trap for us to fall into. Keep your eyes open," Matthieu said, and the rest of us nodded.

As soon as we got our weapons in order, Matthieu led the way across the back alley to a dark house that must have been the Tolberts' place. The back gate was open when we got there, and he stopped.

"See what I told you? I *knew* they went this way," he whispered, pointing at the gate. Nobody said a word while he crept up to the gate and then swiftly stepped inside, swinging his pistol around to cover the whole yard just in case there might be somebody lurking there.

I had to admire the way he did it, I admit; it reminded me of the kind of thing you see on cop shows.

But the yard was empty, and as soon as he was sure it was safe he motioned for the rest of us to come ahead behind him. We did, and the next clue we found was a garage window busted out with a rock.

"Never mind. I think they're already gone. Mrs. Tolbert's car is missing," Jolie said when we got inside.

"Are you sure they're the ones who took it?" I ventured to ask.

"I don't know who else would have. Orem is handy that way; he would have known how to break open the ignition switch and get it started without a key. And I bet they found some old clothes out here in the garage, too. Worse and worse," Matthieu said.

"Any idea where they might have gone from here?" I asked.

"No telling. Like I said, the first thing they'll do is find a place to hole up and hide for a while. They might even split up, for that matter. Andrew knows he's not strong enough to fight us off yet; not without his zombies. I'm sure he thinks we still have the rings at this point," Matthieu said.

"So where's the most *unlikely* place they'd go?" Cameron asked.

There was a pause, and we all glanced together at the Tolberts' house right behind us. It was funny in a way that we all had the same thought at the same instant, and I might have laughed if things hadn't been so serious.

"There's no way they could still be in there. The other car's gone," Matt said in a low voice, looking out at the street.

"Yeah, but we don't know for *sure* it was them who took it, remember? The Tolberts could have taken both cars for some reason. Maybe they had to drop one of them off at the garage to get it fixed or something like that. We don't really know," I pointed out.

Matt frowned, considering the idea.

"Yeah. . . maybe," he finally said, doubtfully.

"We're wasting time. Let's get in there and check it out," Jolie said, and we all nodded.

"Come on, then," Matt said, lowering his pistol and walking back into the garage.

There was nothing much to be seen in there, just a bunch of junk like you'd see in anybody's garage; half empty paint cans, a few tools, a deep freeze, some shelves with various uninteresting things on them. Nothing particularly helpful.

But there were three doors, and those were where we immediately zeroed in. One of them led into the main house, and one of them went upstairs to the guest house on top of the garage. The third one looked like it might be a closet or a storage room, but I wouldn't have sworn to it. Matthieu checked that one first, and inside we found nothing but shelves and boxes full of more junk. We didn't waste ten seconds on it.

The door that led upstairs to the guest house was locked, and it didn't look like anybody had messed with it recently. The one to the main house had nine small panes on the top half of the door, and as soon as we got close enough we noticed that one of them was broken out. It wasn't easy to tell, because whoever broke it had carefully removed all the glass shards to make it look as close to normal as possible.

There was a yellow muslin curtain on the inside that kept us from seeing what was past the door, but Matthieu went up close and listened. There was nothing to hear, so he slowly and carefully tried the knob. Locked.

He quickly slipped his hand through the broken pane just like the Garzas must have done, and turned the knob from inside. Then he opened the door quickly and covered the room with his gun.

Inside was a kitchen; a completely deserted one.

We methodically worked our way through the house, letting Matthieu lead since he was the one who knew what he was doing. But the house was empty and silent, and the only things we noticed were an open drawer in the bedroom and a half-eaten box of granola bars left sitting on the coffee table. Neither of which necessarily meant anything.

"I know they were in here. The door proves that. I bet they took some clothes and ate some food and then left either on foot or in the car," Matthieu said.

I couldn't help thinking there was something we were overlooking, but I couldn't put my finger on what it was till we got back to the kitchen and were just about to leave.

The Tolberts had one of those key holder things hung up on the wall beside the door, with little labels above each hook so you'd know what they were for. Nothing unusual about that, at least not till I noticed the GSTHSE key was missing from its place. As soon as I saw it, I put a hand out to stop Matt.

"Hey, look at that," I said in a low voice.

"What?" he asked.

"The guesthouse key is gone. I bet they took it and that's why we didn't think anybody broke in there," I said. He glanced at the key holder long enough to make sure I was right, and then he nodded.

"All right, makes sense. Let's go find out," he said.

So that's what we did, but almost right away we ran into a problem. The door was locked and the key was missing, and if the Garzas (or some of them) really *were* up there, then we definitely didn't want them to know we were coming.

"Never mind, I can handle this," Matthieu said. He trotted back into the main house, and soon returned with a handful of Mrs. Tolbert's bobby pins. Then we all watched in fascination as he expertly picked the lock. I hadn't known he knew how to do that, but then I guess you have to learn a lot of unusual things when you hunt werewolves and evil sorcerers for a living.

As soon as the lock was done, he raised his pistol and took the lead again, opening the door slowly so there wouldn't be any noise.

Right inside the entrance was a narrow staircase leading steeply up to the guesthouse, and together we slipped our way up there to see what we could see.

It was dark and shadowy inside, and deathly quiet. Matthieu and Jolie went first, and then Cameron came along behind me to make sure we didn't get attacked from the rear. As soon as we made it to the top of the stairs, the first thing we saw was Joan, tied up and gagged on the bed.

But I didn't have time to think about that, because all of a sudden a sword came slicing down on Matthieu's upper arm, knocking the pistol out of his hand and cutting him pretty badly. He staggered backward, knowing he couldn't defend himself against something like that without a weapon, and the dude who swung the sword stepped out of the alcove he'd been hiding in and raised his blade to finish the job.

Maybe he didn't realize there were several of us, but he caught the drift soon enough. Matthieu stumbled into Jolie, knocking her off balance and nearly making both of them fall head over heels down the stairs, right on top of me and Cam. Jolie was in no position to aim very well, but she still had the presence of mind to fire her pistol at the man.

She missed, of course, but the noise was deafening in the hallway and he must have decided the odds weren't in his favor without a gun of his own. He cursed and leaped back behind the doorway so we couldn't see him.

As soon as Jolie caught her balance she quickly fired again three times right through the wall, down low where she might hit the man's legs instead of his body, and we all heard a snarl of pain, followed quickly by the heavy thump of something hitting the floor. She must have nailed somebody pretty good.

Jolie whipped around the corner to cover the man, with me and Cam close behind her. Matthieu had slumped down against the wall and yanked his t-shirt off to wrap up his bleeding arm with, but he was out of commission.

I don't know which one of the Garza brothers it was, but he was lying on the floor glaring at us, still holding the sword in his hand while he tried to put pressure on a bullet wound in his calf. Where in the blessed world he got hold of a sword I'll never know, unless maybe it was some decorative item Mr. Tolbert had put up on the wall or some such thing. I guess anything will do as a weapon in a pinch.

Just then, I felt something crash down on my upper back. I didn't know what it was, but it hurt worse than anything I can ever remember. For a second I thought it was another sword, but whatever it was, it knocked the breath out of me and I fell face-down on the carpet, gasping for air.

I was a little bit dazed after that and I don't entirely remember what happened, but I gathered later on that Gabe had been hiding in the bathroom and he'd come out and hit me with the shower curtain rod. Cameron tackled him from the side and they crashed to the floor, causing the rod itself to hit the carpet six inches in front of my face.

I couldn't help him, and neither could Jolie for that matter. She had her hands full with the wounded one on the floor. He seized the moment of distraction to go for Matthieu's dropped pistol and

Jolie had to blow another hole in the floor beside his arm to make him back off.

Cam is no weakling, but then again neither was Gabe, apparently. He must have decided we had the upper hand, though, and that's when I got my first taste of the Garzas' sorcery. Gabe tore Cam loose and hurled him across the room without using hands, slamming him into the wall beside the bed. Then he took off down the stairs, abandoning his wounded brother. None of us was in any position to stop him, but the upshot of the whole thing was that we collared Orem, at least. Apparently Andrew had never been there to start with. All that takes a long time to tell, but it didn't take more than a few minutes to actually happen.

"Where's Andrew?" Matthieu demanded, after he'd bandaged his arm and got his pistol back. Orem didn't say a word, except to spit on the floor right by his feet.

"Let it alone, Matt. We'll find him sooner or later, anyway. Wherever he is, it's obvious he's not here," Cameron said. He'd earned his share of lumps from the fight; he had a split lip and his nose was bleeding from where his face hit the wall.

"Yeah, I guess you're right. At least we saved the idiot who woke them up in the first place," Matthieu said sourly. He's not usually like that, and I could tell he must have been in considerable pain to make him that curt. I could sympathize; my back was still throbbing from that smack with the curtain rod, and I was sure I'd have a bruise from one side to the other by morning.

I glanced at the bed, where Joan was still bound and gagged. Cameron was already over there from when Gabe had flung him across the room, and since Jolie and Matthieu were both occupied at the moment, I painfully got up and went to help him cut her loose.

She must have been awake the whole time, and I guess she'd probably had a rough few hours. The Garzas had probably been pretty cruel jailers. Her face was dirty, and there were tear streaks where she'd cried and not been able to wipe it away. Some of them looked pretty fresh, in fact, and her eyes were shut when we got to the bed.

"Joan, I know you're awake. You're safe now. Nobody wants to hurt you. I've got a knife and I'm just fixing to cut you loose if you'll be still. If you want to leave after that, you can. We won't try to stop you. But we'd really like to help you if you'll let us," he said.

I saw a tear well up and slide down through the dirt on her cheek, but she nodded. He cut the gag off first.

"There, that's better, now isn't it?" he said soothingly.

Then he cut the girl's hands and legs free, and put his knife away. Joan sat up and opened those leaf-green eyes, looking at the four of us in turn while she rubbed her wrists and ankles.

Chapter Three

"I'm sorry," Joan finally said, looking down at her feet. None of us needed to ask her for what.

"It's all right. Are you okay?" Cam asked, and she gave him a blank look.

"Am I what?" she asked, looking confused. Obviously she'd never heard the word *okay* before.

"Are you all right? Did they hurt you?" he clarified.

"Oh. No, they didn't hurt me. At least not yet," she said, glaring at Orem.

"That's good, at least. I'm not sure what Matthieu wants to do with Dufus over there, but we need to get you out of here, anyway. Not sure how we'd explain where you came from," Cam said, only half joking.

Joan slid to the edge of the bed and glanced at the door with a keen interest.

"I'm ready to leave as soon as we can find a way. What *is* this horrible place?" she asked with a shiver. I didn't know what to say to that. We'd had a similar discussion with the Dolans just a few hours ago, but that was really nothing like this at all. They'd only been asleep for a few years, and Joan had slept for over a hundred and fifty. I didn't even know where to begin. Just like that silly thing about her not understanding the word *okay*. What other surprises were in store?

Cameron must have decided to be as honest as possible, though.

"We're in Natchitoches, Louisiana," he said, and Joan looked at him skeptically.

"It's really true, but it's been a long time since 1864," I said, trying to put it delicately. I tried to think what was going on in Texas that year, so maybe I could figure out some way to relate to what she was going through. I knew the Civil War was raging just about then, but other than that I didn't really have a clue. I wished I'd paid more attention in history class.

"What do you mean, a long time?" she asked.

"Um. . . what's the last thing you remember? I mean, before you woke up with us in the store room?" I asked.

"Why do you ask?" she asked, looking crafty again.

"Oh, for pity's sake, do you still not trust us, even after we just saved your life?" Jolie interrupted from across the room, annoyed. Joan pursed her lips like she wanted to snap back at her, but then she changed her mind.

"All right. I reckon you've earned a few points for that. Sorry. Trust isn't an easy thing for me," she said.

"Okay, well. . . what's the last thing you remember?" I asked again. Joan thought about it, and still looked reluctant.

"It was nighttime, and I was camped alone by the ford on the Sulphur River," she began, and then hesitated, like she thought we might question that. But the only thing that came to mind when I heard about the Sulphur River was that it was a good place to catch catfish, so whatever it was that made her hesitate I don't know. I'm pretty sure it's not because she was afraid of giving away the location of her favorite fishing hole.

"What happened then?" Cam asked.

"Somebody slipped into camp and attacked me. We fought, and that's the last thing I remember," she said.

"That person was named Denis Doucet," Jolie said. I looked closely for any sign of recognition in Joan's eyes, but there was none.

"Who's that?" she asked.

"He was a werewolf hunter," I explained, like it was the most ordinary thing in the world. That got a response. Joan's eyes flew open in shocked surprise, and I saw real fear in her eyes.

"It's all right. That's all over now," Cameron soothed. She didn't look very reassured.

"There are no more werewolves now. They're all cured. Even you," I added.

"We know you used to be one, but we need you to know it doesn't matter anymore," Cam explained. Joan reflexively looked at her fingernails and I had to bite my lip to keep from laughing. I was surprised she hadn't thought to do it before now.

"It seems like I've missed a lot," she murmured.

"You have no idea," I said, and then told her the year.

I wouldn't have been surprised if she'd fainted, but I have to give her credit; she showed the same toughness I'd seen when she first woke up from the dust sleep. I guess she'd seen enough while she was out and about that it didn't cross her mind to doubt me when I said it, but it still took her a minute to wrap her head around the idea that so much time had passed.

"Who won?" she asked, as soon as she'd got herself together. My mind skidded for second and then I realized she must be asking about the Civil War. Of course that would be something that was heavy on her mind, coming from 1864.

On the other hand, she was a Texan and therefore a Confederate, and she wasn't going to like the answer much. But while I was thinking about it, Cameron found a way to finesse the problem.

"It was a terrible thing, but we all made up after a few years and things are better now," he said smoothly, and I couldn't help admiring the deft way he defused what could have turned into an awkward scene. But Joan was only nodding.

"Indeed? Well, no doubt that's for the best," she agreed with a sigh, and then actually seemed to have a sparkle of humor in her eyes.

"What is it?" I asked, not sure what was so funny.

"Well, I don't suppose it matters anymore, but I was a scout for the Confederate army," she said, with a smile.

That seemed hard to believe; I didn't think they let girls join the army back then.

"You were?" I asked skeptically.

"Yeah. They laughed at me when I went down to the post to volunteer, but then after I showed the commander what I could do, he was more than happy to let me help. I was the best scout they had," she said proudly.

No doubt she had been, I thought to myself. A wolf would've made an excellent scout, especially if she got some stealth and weapons training. That also explained how she was able to sneak up on us and listen to our conversation in the store room without anybody noticing. She was a spy.

Or at least she used to be, anyway. I wondered idly if there was any way for her to collect a hundred and fifty years worth of back pay from the Army. She'd probably be richer than the Doucets.

"That's awesome," Cameron said, and she smiled.

"Maybe it used to be, but I'm not sure what to do with myself, now," she said, the smile slowly fading from her lips.

"We'll help you figure it out," he said, and I couldn't help but notice the admiration in his voice when he said it. Cam has always had a thing for strong girls, even though he'd never admit it. But he was asking for trouble, flirting with one from such a different past and who had such an uncertain future. I suppose beauty is still beautiful no matter what the circumstances, but still, I decided to have a serious talk with him at the first available opportunity.

"Matthieu says we need to leave before the cops get here in a few minutes. He said he'll guard Orem till then," Jolie said, interrupting my train of thought. That didn't sound like such a great idea to me, not with his arm nearly chopped off like it was, but I didn't say anything about it. Matthieu usually has good reasons for the things he does, and I figured he probably had one this time, too.

So that's what we did, and before long we were sitting in Sarah Doucet's kitchen again, only this time with Joan in tow.

She seemed awed by the electric lights and all the other trinkets in the house, as full of wonder as a baby. It really makes you think, you know; we take so much for granted that we hardly ever remember anymore that even the poorest of us is richer than a king would have been just a couple hundred years ago. It's kind of humbling.

In fact she was fascinated by *everything,* from TV and telephones to plastic and air conditioning. Even little things like zippers and toothpaste were a source of unending amazement for her. We kept forgetting how much she didn't know. I guess I'd never thought about when zippers and toothpaste were invented; those are the kinds of things you tend to think have been around forever, you know? But apparently not.

In fact, she wanted to eat the toothpaste the first time she tasted any, and we had to show her how to use it like you'd show a three-year-old.

She was still wearing the gray sweats we'd put on her when she first woke up, and after a while Jolie looked at her critically.

"Come on, girl. Let's go find you something nicer to wear than that. I'm sure Aunt Sarah probably has some clothes you could use for the time being," she said.

Joan nodded and the two of them left the room together, leaving me alone with Cameron for the first time in hours.

"Cam, there's something I was meaning to talk to you about when we had some time," I began carefully.

"Yeah? What's that?" he asked.

"Well, it sure does seem like you and Joan are getting along real well," I said, and he laughed.

"So you think me and her might have some little thing going on, is that it?" he asked, smiling.

"The thought did cross my mind," I admitted.

"No, it's nothing like that, Zach, honestly. I like her as a person, but she's way too old for me, you know," he said.

"You're exactly the same age, Cam," I pointed out, refusing to get sidetracked by any stupid jokes about how old she was.

"Well, yeah, maybe so. But it's not like it's anything serious. I just like her, that's all. I like lots of people," he said.

"Just be careful, bro, that's all I'm saying. She grew up a lot different than we did," I said.

"I know," he said, trying to be serious about it.

It wasn't long before the girls came back into the kitchen. Joan was wearing a dress this time; a long green one that came down almost to her ankles and had blue flowers on it. It was pretty, but awfully antique-looking. It reminded me of something an old Amish lady might wear to church on a day when she felt like getting specially dressed up, honestly. She'd washed her face and put her hair down and brushed it, and she had on some black moccasins.

Cam whistled at her again, and she smiled. I wanted to glare at him, considering that we'd just finished discussing that very subject, but I didn't.

Maybe it shouldn't have worried me so much, but unfortunately I know Cameron too well. He varies between being quiet and shy sometimes and then switching gears to lighthearted and fun-loving, but he wears his heart on his sleeve and he falls in love at the drop of a hat. You'd never guess it if you didn't know him, but he does. He was hung up on Janie Johnston for months after he kissed her at the fair last year at the kissing booth. She must have liked it, because she flirted with him a little bit afterward and gave him an extra kiss for free. Nobody could blame her, I don't guess. After you've had to kiss flabby old dudes and geeky dorks with onion breath all day, a good-looking young country boy was probably Heaven-sent, as far as she was concerned.

But it didn't do Cameron any good at all. He never told anybody how he felt, but like I said, I know him too well. I don't think Janie ever even knew about it. And truthfully I'm glad she didn't. I don't think she would've been interested in him anyway, and even if she had been, I think she would have made his life miserable. She was too wild and careless.

Joan was made of much finer stuff, to be sure. She had a core of steel under that pretty exterior, but I still didn't know her well enough to draw any conclusions about how she and Cameron might get along. Let alone the fact that he was twice her size; well over a foot taller and probably almost a hundred pounds heavier, and couples always look a little strange when that happens. I was willing to suspend judgment for a while, but still, it worried me.

But while I was thinking about all that, the conversation had moved on without me.

"This was all I could get her to wear. She said everything else in the closet was indecent," Jolie said.

"It was! I can't believe proper young ladies would wear clothes like that," Joan said.

"It's like I told you, dear. In this time and place, people have a different idea about proper clothes than they did in 1864. I promise I wouldn't dress you like a shameless hussy," Jolie said.

"I believe you, but some of those dresses, they look like, like. . . " Joan said, and shook her head ruefully.

"Yeah, I know what it probably looks like, coming from where you come from, but trust me on this, okay?" Jolie told her.

"I guess there's no chance I could ever go back home, is there?" she asked, with a wistful tone in her voice.

"No, I'm afraid not. But we'll do the best we can to help you make a life for yourself here," Jolie said gently.

"I wouldn't mind so much, if I hadn't left my sister back there. I guess whatever's done is done by now, but it sure is hard to get used to the idea that she's gone," she said sadly.

"But she-" I began, fully meaning to tell her that Annabelle was still sitting out there in a misplaced bottle somewhere in the store room. But just about then, Matthieu opened the door and came back inside.

"Is Orem gone?" I asked immediately, forgetting about Annabelle Rusk for the time being.

"Locked up tight as a jug in the parish jail. Assault, battery, breaking and entering, terroristic threatening, maybe even a few other things. He won't be getting out any time soon, that's for sure," he said.

"I don't know how you did it, Matt," I said, shaking my head.

"You'd be amazed how much having the right name can help you get things done in this town," he said cryptically.

"He means our family has enough money and influence that sometimes we can pull a few strings when we need to. He just doesn't like to say so," Jolie explained.

Matthieu didn't answer, and I couldn't think of anything to say, either. Maybe it shouldn't have surprised me, but I'd never realized Jolie and Matthieu had enough pull to get somebody thrown in jail without bond just on their say-so.

And maybe they didn't, really. It wasn't like the Garzas were innocent little lambs or anything. They'd done plenty to get themselves in hot water. But it was still pretty amazing that the cops would take Matt's word for what happened and not even ask any questions. He might have been a Doucet, but he was still only nineteen years old.

"Looks like you'll need some stitches in that arm, Matt," Jolie said. It was still bound up in his t-shirt, but the fabric was soaked with blood and it had started to drip on the floor even in the short time since he'd come into the kitchen. Matt sighed.

"Yeah, I'm sure I do. The cops wanted to call an ambulance to take me down to the emergency room, but I said no. I didn't want to cause any more of a scene out there at the Tolberts' than we already did. But yeah, I'd appreciate it if one of y'all would take me," he said.

"I'll do it. Why don't the rest of you stay here and make sure the house is safe, okay?" Jolie said.

"Sure," I said, and the others nodded.

She wrapped up Matthieu's arm in a towel so it wouldn't drip any more blood on the floor, and then grabbed the keys to her bug. We followed them to the front door and made sure it was locked as soon as they left. I wondered for a second how many sword cuts they had to treat at the hospital in Natchitoches. I was sure the two of them could come up with some kind of convincing explanation for how it happened, but still. . .

I ducked into the bathroom and took some ibuprofen tablets from the medicine cabinet to dull the pain from my back, and by the time I got back to the kitchen, Cam had already been outside to lock the back gate and the store room door. I guess he had Gabe and Andrew on his mind, just like I did. I felt better with the house locked up tight; nobody was getting past the security system in *that* house. True, me and Cameron had slipped in through the chimney a few months ago, but Sarah Doucet had closed up even that loophole the minute she found out about it. There might still be other ways in that nobody had thought of yet, but I hoped not.

We made a pot of spaghetti and some garlic bread for supper, which was another thing Joan had apparently never heard of before. She eyed the food suspiciously before she took a bite, and I don't think she really liked it very much. She scraped most of the meat sauce to the side of her plate and just ate the noodles and cheese. She wouldn't touch the garlic bread at all.

That was all right, though, because I helped myself to the leftovers. No reason to let it go to waste, after all. She did drink the milk and asked for seconds on that, so I guess that was one thing she must have been used to having.

After we cleared the table we went into the living room and watched a movie, which fascinated Joan to no end after we explained that it wasn't real.

Jolie and Matthieu were still gone by the time we started getting sleepy, so we gave Joan one of the spare bedrooms and left her alone for the night. Me and Cam were supposed to be bunking down with Matthieu in his room, but I still wanted to stay up for a little while to see if the others would make it back. I would have called, but I knew cell phones were off limits in the hospital. Besides that, my back still hurt and I doubted I'd be able to sleep very well, anyway.

Cam sat up with me for a little while, more out of duty than because he really wanted to, I think. He was tired; I could see it from the way his eyes drooped.

"Go to bed, bro. I know you're tired. I'll be up there in a little bit," I finally told him.

"You sure?" he asked.

"Yeah, I'm sure. Go ahead," I told him.

So he did, and I found myself sitting downstairs on the couch in the big silent house, with only the hum of the refrigerator to keep me company.

I almost dozed off, to tell the truth. I must have been more tired than I thought. But the vibration of my cell phone snapped me awake. I didn't recognize the number, but I answered it anyway. It was Jolie, calling from the hospital.

"Hey, Blue-Eyes. I didn't wake you, did I?" she asked.

"No, I'm still up. How's Matthieu?"

"That was a pretty nasty slice he got. They had to do surgery on his arm to stitch the muscles back together. They said he'll be all right in a few weeks; it'll just hurt in the meantime. Anyway, we'll probably be home in about an hour. He's pretty doped up but I think he'll be all right," she said.

"I'm glad he's okay," I said.

"Yeah, me too. But Matt's pretty tough when he has to be," she agreed.

"I was kinda worried about you, babe, being out there on the streets with the Garzas still loose somewhere," I told her.

"I'm sure they're long gone by now, but we'll be careful, I promise. You should go to bed in the meantime, though; I know you're sleepy. I can hear it in your voice," she said.

"I'd feel better if you got home, first," I said, and she laughed a little.

"Yeah, I love you too, Blue-Eyes. But go to bed, honestly. For me? Please?" she asked, and finally I had to laugh.

"Maybe I will," I agreed.

"All right. Good night, baby. Love you," she said.

"Love you too," I told her, and that was it.

I took some more pain pills before dragging myself upstairs to Matthieu's room. That's where me and Cam usually sleep whenever we stay the night in Natchitoches, cause it's fun to sit up late and socialize till you pass out without having to get up and find somewhere else to crash at the last minute. He's got a set of bunk beds in his room and a big fluffy couch that are perfect for that kind of thing.

Cam was already asleep on the couch with his mouth yawped open, drooling on his pillow. I put on some shorts and climbed into the top bunk, trying to lie on my side so it wouldn't bother my back quite as much. It hurt so much I was sure I'd be awake all night long.

I was asleep in ten seconds flat.

I don't remember when Matt came in and crawled into bed. He must not have made very much noise. The next thing I remember it was daylight outside, and the others were both still asleep.

I climbed out of bed and got dressed, feeling a sharp stab of pain now and then from the bruise on my back. You wouldn't think a curtain rod could be such a deadly weapon, would you?

I tried to be quiet, but Matthieu is a light sleeper. He opened his eyes and looked at me when I was slipping my shoes on.

"Hey, how's your arm?" I asked. He grimaced.

"It's been better, that's for sure," he admitted, sitting up in bed. He held it up for me to see, and it was wrapped in white bandages almost all the way from his shoulder to his elbow. Just a little higher and Orem might have chopped the boy's head off. No sooner did the thought cross my mind than my overactive imagination obligingly supplied me with a hideous image of exactly what that would look like.

"Hope you get to feeling better," I said, feeling a little green from imagining Matthieu with no head. I decided it was definitely time to think about something else, before I ruined my appetite.

Jolie must have decided to cook that morning, because there were flaky biscuits and sausage gravy on the stove when I got to the kitchen, with a tray of cantaloupe and watermelon wedges on the side. She was sitting at the kitchen table herself, nibbling on a slice of cantaloupe. I said good morning and gave her a kiss as I walked by, and then helped myself to a big plate of food.

I didn't want to think about the Garzas, hard as it was to keep from it. They were a looming danger who would almost certainly cause us some serious grief before we could capture them again, but that couldn't be helped. At least Orem was out of the picture.

"Did you sleep okay last night? With your back, I mean?" Jolie asked, between bites of cantaloupe.

"Better than I thought I would," I said, feeling another twinge. It was better than yesterday, but it still hurt.

There wasn't time to say anything else, because Matthieu showed up just then. He quietly helped himself to some breakfast before sitting down at the table across from me.

"I've been thinking," he said, his mouth full of biscuit.

"About what?" I asked.

"What to do about the Garzas, of course," he said.

"You had to mention that at breakfast, didn't you," Jolie sighed, shaking her head. I knew how she felt; it was the proverbial eight hundred pound gorilla in the room which nobody wants to mention, but we had to figure something out, and soon.

Chapter Four

"I know it's a thorny problem, but we've got to talk about it sometime," Matthieu pointed out.

"The problem is, we don't know what *they* might do. It's hard to make plans when you don't know anything," Jolie said.

"Well, I'm sure that little episode last night was nothing but a diversion. I bet Andrew is the one who took Mrs. Tolbert's car and left the other two there with Joan to keep us busy for a while. He wouldn't have cared what happened to *them,* as long as he saved his own skin; no more than Gabe cared what happened to Orem," he said.

"Why would they do what he said, then?" I asked.

"Mostly because he'd fry them both to ashes if they didn't," Matthieu said coolly. That was a good reason, but it was also an unwelcome reminder of what brutal thugs these people were.

"So what now, then?" I asked.

"I'm not near as worried about Gabe right now as I am Andrew. *He's* the really dangerous one, and like I told you last night, I'm pretty sure I know exactly what *he'll* do. He'll run to ground in a place he's got no connections to, somewhere we'd never think of. Then he'll lay low and start building up his power for a while, killing folks in lonely spots, stealing their money and turning them into zombies. Then when he thinks he's strong enough, he'll come after us. But he probably won't do that for a good long time, yet; not till he's sure he can win. He's smart, though; he might do something totally unexpected, too," he said.

"You're not worried about Gabe at all?" I asked.

"I wouldn't go so far as to say that. But he was never the ringleader, so I didn't study him near as much. I do know he and Andrew don't get along very well, though. If I had to guess, I'd say that Gabe will probably use this as an opportunity to get away from Andrew and do his own thing for a while. But as for what that might involve, I don't know enough to say. He may never attack us or even show his face again, for all I know. But I'm *certain* Andrew will. You can bet on that much," he said.

"We can't just let them roam around free like that," I said, and Matt shrugged.

"I honestly can't think of any way to stop them, Zach; not till they show themselves again," he said, shaking his head.

Matthieu had a point, much as I hated to admit it. When you've got absolutely no idea where to start searching, then you might as well give up on the idea of finding somebody. The world is just too big of a place. It would have taken a miracle to find Gabe or Andrew either one.

"You don't think either one of them might stay in town and try to help Orem?" I asked, and Matthieu snorted.

"I told you, Zach, none of them ever does anything unless it benefits them personally. Orem could rot in jail for the rest of his life for all they care," he said.

"But wouldn't it benefit them to bust out their best flunky?" I persisted.

"Sure, if they didn't get caught in the process. But alone, in a strange town, with no money and nowhere to run? I don't think so. They won't bother with Orem unless the benefits outweigh the risks, and right now they don't. They're awfully practical that way," Matthieu said.

The conversation had made us gloomy, and I decided maybe it was time to change the subject.

"All right, I guess we'll just have to cross our fingers and pray for the best when it comes to Andrew and Gabe, then. But what about the rest of the sleepers?" I asked.

"What about them?" Jolie asked.

"Well, I assume the project to wake up the rest of them is still on track, isn't it?" I asked.

"I don't know about that, Zach. Maybe we should wait a little while, till we figure out what to do about the Garzas. It won't matter to the sleepers if they have to wait a little while longer. Besides, we've already got one of them to have to deal with," he pointed out.

"Yeah, true," I agreed. I guess I forgot about Joan for a while.

"I do think one thing we need to do is move the store room elsewhere, at least for a while. Preferably not even in Natchitoches. The Garzas know how to find this house, and we can't risk letting them have access to all those people," Matthieu said.

"You don't think we could just move them down to the basement here?" I asked.

"We *could*, but I'd feel safer if they didn't know where anything was at all. Yeah, we've got the security system, but nothing like that is ever perfect. You and Cam found a way in here without too much trouble, and y'all are not even experts," Matthieu pointed out.

"What do you think they could do, though? They wouldn't be able to wake up any of them without some water," I said.

"Maybe not, but if nothing else they might go in there and smash all the bottles and dump them on the floor, just for spite. Don't think they wouldn't do it, either. Or who knows? Andrew is pretty smart; he might find a way to wake up a few of them, after all. We know one way to do it, but we don't know that it's the *only* way," Matthieu said.

"No, it's not the only way. Marc said you could do it if you killed somebody else and mixed all their blood with the dust," Jolie said.

"Well, there you go. I doubt Gabe would ever think to try it, but Andrew wouldn't hesitate to do something like that, if he thought it helped him. And it very well might; some of the people in there are almost as bad as he is," Matt said.

"That's a lot of bottles to move," I said doubtfully.

"Yeah, but it's not as bad as you might think. They're small, so they pack down pretty good," Matthieu said.

We decided after much debate to hide the bottles at Miss Edith's old place in Red Lick for a while. It was a place the Garzas knew nothing about, it was far from Natchitoches, and it had the added advantage of being close to the supply of sweet water. Plus, me and Cam were close enough to keep an eye on the place pretty regularly. It seemed like the ideal solution. None of us expected to leave the sleepers there forever, of course, if only because of the simple fact that we'd hopefully be waking them up soon.

Most of the morning we spent packing the bottles into cardboard boxes, being very careful not to break any of them. Each box held about fifty bottles more or less, and by the time we were done we had forty-three boxes full. Then we packed them up in the bed of Matthieu's truck along with the file cabinet that held the information on all those pods. Counting them all up, there were 2,193 ex-wolves in that store room, enough to fill up a sizable little town.

I drove us from Natchitoches to Red Lick, since I was the one who knew the way best. I parked the truck behind Miss Edith's house so no one could see it from the highway if they drove by, and then we spent another hour or so hauling the boxes down to the cellar. We had to rearrange the shelves to make everything fit, and it was such a tight squeeze that we ended up having to shove the file cabinet up under the stairs. But that was all right, though; everything was safely stowed, and that was all that mattered.

"I think you should drink a little of this, for your arm," I said, offering Matthieu a bottle of sweet water. I try not to use it except for things that are life-threatening, which Matt's injury wasn't. But then on the other hand, there were the Garzas to think about, and Matthieu was our most seasoned fighter. The survival of all of us might depend on whether he was in good shape or not.

He knew that himself, of course, so he didn't quibble about saving the water for more important things. He just nodded and took a sip from the bottle, and such was the power of that holy spring that within minutes the sword-cut had vanished completely. It's awesome to see it happen even now, even for me. I took a sip of it myself for similar reasons, and felt the bruise on my back disappear like it was never there.

By then it was pushing one o'clock, and me and Cam had to get to work. Mr. Barling is pretty easygoing about exactly what time we get there, as long as we finish everything we're supposed to do. He owns the Hope ranch down in the Red River bottoms, and mostly raises Hereford cows, praline pecans, and alfalfa hay. We worked with all those things from time to time, but early June is mostly hay-day, so to speak. The fields were already mowed and dry when we got there, so we hooked up the baler to the tractor and spent most of the afternoon baling it up into little square bales and then moving them to the barn. I like that kind of work, even though it was hot outside and dry grass is sharper than you would think. You almost always end up with little hay-cuts all over your arms by the time the day is done.

I was tired and sweaty by the time we got finished, not to mention hungry. I called Jolie to come get us, and she drove over there in Matthieu's truck to pick us up. I made a beeline for the shower as soon as we got back to Miss Edith's house, and then rubbed some cornhuskers lotion on my arms to keep the hay-cuts from stinging so much.

Matthieu ordered pizza since it was almost suppertime, and as soon as it was delivered we all sat around the big oak dining table and clinked our glasses to a job well done.

Joan had never heard of pizza before, naturally, but after we coaxed her to try some she quickly decided that was one food she really liked. She'd never tried Coke before, either, and she didn't like that at all, so she ended up drinking water instead. Water and pizza doesn't seem like a very tasty combination to me, but I didn't comment.

We stayed at Miss Edith's house that night, since it was getting late and nobody wanted to drive all the way back to Natchitoches. Me and Cam could have gone home, I guess, but I didn't feel right leaving Matt and Jolie and Joan to rough it in Red Lick. It's not that Miss Edith's house was uncomfortable or anything; it was just an old lady's house, and you could tell it the second you walked in the door. You know what I mean; there's just something about the décor, and the odor, and the choice of furniture. I'm not sure what it is, but you always know. I'd never spent the night there before, but there's a first time for everything, they say.

"How's Joan doing?" I asked Jolie when we had a few minutes together before bedtime.

"Better than she was. I convinced her to take a bath and brush her teeth today," she said.

"Well, that's good at least," I said.

"I told her Cameron would like it a lot better if she did," she said, and I laughed.

"Oh, you noticed that too, did you? He swears up and down there's nothing to it, but I don't believe him. He talks about her too much for it to be nothing," I said.

"She asked me if he was interested in anybody, so I think it's mutual," she said.

"Well, I guess that's between him and her. I have my doubts about whether it's wise or not, but I already told him that once and I won't pester him about it," I said.

"Aw, I think it's sweet. Cameron is a good dude. And whatever else she may be, I know Joan is a believer and I know she's loyal. She's really a very nice person once you get to know her a little. I think they might be good for each other," she said.

"Maybe. I just worry that she might not see things the way we do, since she grew up so different. But I guess you never know. We'll see what happens," I said.

As it turned out, that was to be the first and the last night I ever spent under Miss Edith's roof, although I went to bed completely unaware of what was coming. I just remember the sound of the crickets outside on the lawn, and hearing Jolie laugh at something Matthieu said down the hall, and feeling glad to be with my friends and the people I loved, in spite of whatever danger might be coming.

I only wish it could have lasted a while longer.

I was wakened sometime during the night by the loudest blast I've ever heard in my life, and I literally felt myself torn right out of bed and hurled against the wall so hard I swear I felt bones crack. I crashed to the floor in a heap, feeling wood and glass and who-knew-what else falling all over me, and then came a wave of heat so intense that I thought it would fry me alive.

I could barely see and barely move, and I'm pretty sure the only reason I survived at all is because there was a window not three feet from where I lay. I honestly don't think I could have made it any farther than that. I crawled out through the shattered glass, cutting my hands and about to pass out from pain and smoke and heat. I fell onto the grass and crawled a few more feet before I collapsed on the lawn, and that was the last I knew.

When I woke up, I couldn't move. Not because they had me restrained or anything; I was just so weak I couldn't have lifted a finger if I'd wanted to. My head felt thick and dopey, and I knew in a vague kind of way that my body would have been hurting a lot if I hadn't been drugged.

I seemed to be in a hospital, from what I could tell. The whole world was nothing but white and chrome, with things beeping and flashing and tubes and cords running everywhere. I thought at first I was alone, but then I flicked my eyes far enough to the side that I caught sight of Eileen, sitting in an armchair beside my bed. She was staring at a book, not really reading it, and it looked like she might have been crying. Now if you know anything about Eileen Wilder, you'd know she's just about the last person on earth who's apt to cry about anything. I think seeing her like that scared me worse than waking up and finding myself in the hospital.

I managed to open my eyes a little more and gave a tiny croak; the best sound I could manage. Eileen looked at me instantly.

"Zach, are you awake?" she asked, and I blinked. I wanted to ask her what happened, but I didn't have the energy for that. Nevertheless, I guess she knew me well enough to know that I'd want to know.

"There was an explosion; the police think somebody planted a bomb under the house. The whole place was completely destroyed. It's a miracle any of you survived; it was even on the news. You've got three broken ribs and a concussion, and you were burned pretty badly over a big part of your body. They didn't know for sure if you'd make it or not. Cam was burned even worse than you; Justin's with him right now, but he still hasn't woken up, yet. Jolie got out with a broken wrist and a few cuts and bruises, and Matthieu got two broken legs and some pretty bad burns on his lower body, too; they say he might lose them. That other girl, she didn't get hurt too much, but she pulled Cameron and Matthieu out before they burned to death. I took her home with me and Justin, so she's fine," she told me.

I hardly cared how badly hurt I seemed to be, when I heard those words about Miss Edith's house being blown to smithereens. That meant no more water, and even worse, it meant the end of all those thousands of people we just moved to the cellar. I could only pray that the explosion hadn't shattered or melted every bottle in the place. Even if there was nothing left but a smoking pile of rubble, the very first thing we'd have to do when we got out of the hospital was dig down and see if there was anything left. From the way Eileen talked, it didn't sound very promising.

I was relieved that Jolie was all right, but it seemed like Matthieu and Cam were even worse off than I was. I was grateful beyond words that Joan had saved them, but the whole experience must have scared her half to death, especially with all those sirens blaring and lights flashing; stuff she never imagined in her worst nightmares. She'd proved she could take care of herself, but she was in no condition to handle the modern world just yet.

I wondered how long I'd be in the hospital, and I thought uneasily about all those burns and whether they might leave really bad scars. It's not that I'm vain or anything, but I didn't want to come out looking like Freddy Krueger, you know. But I couldn't ask, and Eileen didn't see fit to mention it.

"Don't worry, baby; it'll be all right. One of us will stay here with you the whole time when they'll let us, but I want you to rest and sleep as much as you can, so you'll get better," she said.

Eileen doesn't usually call me "baby" very much, either, and I wondered if she thought I was dying. Who knows; maybe I was. But I was too tired and beginning to hurt too much to care, and I guess she saw the pain on my face.

"I'll tell them to give you some morphine, okay? It'll put you to sleep, but I promise I'll still be here when you wake up," she said.

And that's what she did. She called the nurse and had her give me a big shot of morphine, which knocked out the pain almost instantly but also left me irresistibly drowsy. So I gave in to sleep, and for a long time I knew no more.

The rest of the day went by like that, long stretches of drugged-out sleep punctuated by brief periods of being awake and mostly in pain. I did get marginally stronger, at least enough that I could talk a little bit or take a sip of juice now and then. Any more than that was beyond me.

Jolie came to see me the next morning with her wrist in a cast and a long, ugly scratch across her face from her left ear to the tip of her chin; it looked like it might leave a permanent mark, and her hair was all singed and burned in places.

"Was it the Garzas?" I asked her, and she nodded.

"We think so. They've always enjoyed bombs, but we're almost certain this one was Andrew's doing. He builds things which are a lot more sophisticated than anything Gabe would ever come up with, let alone Orem. That's how this one was; lots of complex circuitry. I was afraid he might do something unexpected like that; he's good at surprises," she sighed.

"Do you think he'll come to the hospital and try to finish us off?" I asked, alarmed at the thought.

"He would, if he thought he could get away with it. But he's probably waiting to see whether y'all survive or not before he takes that risk. I don't think you realize how bad off the others really are, Zach. They're both awake now, but severe burns are really dangerous things. I'm sure Dr. Garza has his ways of knowing things, though, and if he ever gets the idea that any of you is certain to live, then I'm sure it won't be long before he shows up at the hospital. That's one reason why we've always made sure somebody is with you and Cam and Matt at all times. We don't dare let him slip in here and find you unguarded, not even for a few minutes," she said.

That was a terrifying thought, actually; I could imagine Andrew coming into the room to put me out of my misery while I was helpless even to raise a hand to defend myself. Jolie, of course, was trained in martial arts and fighting techniques and probably knew how to use a plastic bedpan as a deadly weapon in a pinch if she had to. Even with a broken wrist, she was a tough customer.

Just then, there came a knock on the door.

My heart dropped to my feet, and I didn't say a word. I couldn't have got up off that bed to save my life, and I knew it. But the door opened in spite of my silence, and instead of Andrew Garza, in came Joan Rusk, probably the last person on earth I would have expected right then.

"Joan?" I asked, wondering if my eyes were working right.

"Yeah, it's me. We don't have time to talk, though. Drink this," she said, and the sweetheart actually pulled a plastic bottle of water out of her pocket. Somehow I knew what it was without needing to ask.

"Is that what I think it is?" I asked.

"Yeah. Sorry it took me so long but I couldn't get down there to the cellar any sooner than this morning. But here, drink. Both of you," she said, offering it to us.

I took a sip of the water, savoring its sweetness, and within minutes I felt new life flowing down every finger and toe. I sat up in bed, reaching for my side where I supposedly had three broken ribs. I couldn't have done that ten minutes ago; not without excruciating pain, at least. But now they seemed good as new. Then I reached down to feel my legs where the worst burns had been. They were gone. I glanced at Jolie, standing there watching me. I couldn't tell if she still had a broken wrist or not, but it sure didn't look like it. The scratch on her face was gone, and even her singed hair seemed good as new. She didn't have so much as a nick or a cut anywhere, and I soon realized that neither did I.

I took a deep breath, to test my ribs and make sure they were really healed. Then I swung my feet around and put them on the floor.

"You better get dressed, Zach. I've still got to fix the others," Joan said.

"But how?" I asked, still lost in the wonder of it all.

"I'll tell you later, but there's no time right now. Dr. Garza is on his way up here *right now,*" she said.

That was enough to get me moving, and I hastily grabbed a shirt and jeans from the closet and pulled them on, not caring a bit about modesty or even tearing my bandages off. Joan didn't wait; she went immediately to give a sip of water to Cameron and Matthieu, and then as soon as possible we all ran headlong down the exit stairs. Matt didn't even have his shoes on because of the casts on both his legs, and had to hobble along with me and Cam to help him.

We somehow made it down to the parking lot and took cover in the scrubby pine woods across from the hospital. Only when we were completely out of sight did Joan let us slow down.

Chapter Five

"I think we're safe here, for a minute at least," she said.

"How'd you get here, anyway?" I asked.

"Your friend Levi came by the house this morning to check on you. I asked him to drop me off out in Red Lick, since I didn't know whether he knew about the water or not. Then I fetched a bottle and walked the rest of the way," she shrugged, and I made a note to myself to fall down and kiss Levi's feet next time I saw him. He was a life-saver. Literally.

Then the rest of what she said registered.

"You walked all the way here from *Red Lick?*" I asked, hardly believing it. That was ten miles or more; a long slog even for an army scout.

"Yeah," she agreed, like it was nothing. I thought of those stories you hear about how people in the old days had to walk five miles to school every day, barefoot in the snow and uphill in both directions. Maybe there's some truth to it after all.

"So what happened?" Matthieu asked, speaking for all of us.

"They had a report on the news this morning after Justin and Eileen went to work, about how all three of you were expected to survive at this point, so when Levi showed up I decided I couldn't wait any longer. The coals at the house were still hot when I got there, so I had to carry water from the well and pour it on some of the worst spots before I could get through to see if there was anything to be salvaged. It was ticklish business, but I finally managed to grab a broken bottle that wasn't completely spilled," she said.

"You actually went back in the house?" I asked.

"I had to. I knew Dr. Garza wouldn't hesitate to finish the job while he still could, as soon as he heard that news report. I had to get y'all out of there," she said.

"How did you know he'd do that?" Jolie asked.

"It's what I'd do," Joan said, and I flinched at the cold-bloodedness of the statement.

"I'm impressed," Cameron said, and she smiled.

"How did you know Dr. Garza was on his way, though?" I asked.

"I saw him getting out of his car in the parking lot, that's how; I'd recognize that man's face anywhere. And it's lucky for all of you that I did. We probably just barely missed him," she said.

"He'll know we couldn't have left very much before he got there. All he has to do is ask the nurses," Matthieu said.

"Right, so that means we better get out of here as fast as we can," I said.

"Let's get these bandages off first, so you won't stick out so much. We don't want him to be able to follow us if we can help it," Joan said, and that was good sense. We ripped loose everything we could tear off, but that still left Matthieu with casts on both legs.

"I've got to get these things off," he muttered.

"We've got to get a car before we even *think* about anything else," Jolie said.

"Whatever we do, we can't stay here. Dr. Garza has probably already found out we're gone. We've got to get a move on," Joan said.

"What about the hospital? Won't they wonder where we went, too?" I asked.

"Yeah, we'll have to call and tell them we had a ballgame we couldn't miss. Wonder what they'd think about that," Cam said, laughing a little. It wasn't all that funny, but sometimes you have to find your humor where you can.

"The mall is right over there across the interstate. That's the closest place I know of where we can call a taxi. All the rest of these places are banks and offices and we don't have time to haggle with them about using the phone," Matthieu said.

So we cut across to where Cowhorn Creek dives under the interstate, and slogged our way through the tunnel. The creek itself was almost dry, which helped, and it had the advantage of keeping us out of sight. We kept following the creek past a baseball field and then through a belt of trees, and finally we were there.

"We sure are filthy, to be going in the mall," Jolie said, and it was true. We had dirt and mud all over us from our short trek along the creek bed.

"Are you seriously worried about how we look?" I asked skeptically.

"I am if they ask us to leave because of it," she said.

"As long as we get to use the phone first I don't care if they ask us to leave. Come on," Matthieu said.

We went inside, and they did at least have a wheelchair so we didn't have to help Matt hobble along on his casts anymore. Nobody asked us to leave, but we did get a few strange looks from some of the other customers. I wanted to cringe every time somebody stared at us, not because I cared what they thought but because I knew that was one more person who might remember something odd and be able to tell Dr. Garza later on if he came snooping around.

Matthieu immediately bought a disposable phone and called a taxi, and while we waited for it to get there he also took the opportunity to stop by an ATM machine and get some cash.

We were on pins and needles the whole time, expecting Dr. Garza to show up any minute, but thankfully that didn't happen. The taxi pulled in to the curb and we got inside, and Matthieu had the driver take us to a used car lot on the other side of town. Jolie was right about needing transportation; being on foot put us at a major disadvantage.

I've never seen anybody write a check for a car before, I have to admit. I think the dealer was pretty skeptical too, for that matter, especially when the check-writer was a nineteen year old boy in muddy clothes, bare feet, and casts on both his legs. Matthieu just shrugged and told him to call the bank if he felt like it. He did, and after that his attitude changed considerably. Matthieu didn't seem to notice or care, but it was pretty funny to me.

I don't even remember what kind of car it was; some big nondescript-looking boat that was big enough to hold all five of us and had tinted windows and a good air conditioner. It was gray and it was a Ford, that's all I know.

Jolie drove, and soon we found a trucker's clinic where they were able to cut the casts off Matthieu's legs. I don't know what he told them when he went back there, but when he came back out he was on two feet again.

"I guess we better go out to Red Lick and see what's left before we leave town. We might need some more water, if things like this keep happening," Matthieu said reluctantly.

"You don't think Dr. Garza would look for us there?" Cameron asked.

"No. He's got no reason to think we'd go back there. He never knew about the water, or at least I don't think he did. We're as safe there as we are anywhere else," Matthieu said gloomily.

Nobody objected, so Jolie silently took us out there and parked the car in the front yard of Miss Edith's house. Or what was left of it, I should say. There were bits and pieces of wood and glass all over the yard, and the house itself had been blown to pieces. It seemed that most of the blast had gone in one direction, blowing out the west side of the structure and causing that part to collapse completely. The five of us had been sleeping on the side that only got the milder part of the explosion, and I shuddered to think what might have happened if Dr. Garza had placed the bomb so it was facing a different angle. We might all have been killed instantly, as he no doubt intended. The impact had been bone-crushing as it was.

There'd been more fire than I thought. No doubt it was that initial surge of heat from the bomb that burned all of us so badly, but everything was scorched and in places even charred. In fact it was still smoking in places, and I could feel the heat radiating from it even from twenty feet away.

What was left of the house looked like it might collapse at any moment, probably killing anybody who was foolish enough to be inside. The door to the cellar was still visible, though, half hidden behind a pile of debris.

"Looks pretty dangerous," Matthieu commented, and I had to agree. Joan had been insane to go down there.

"Yeah, but we've got to have some water," I said grimly.

I was probably insane myself, but I ever-so-slowly made my way across the wrecked living room, listening to the hulk of wood above me creak and rattle even in the mild breeze. Once a piece of blackened wood fell and landed right in front of me, causing my heart to skip a beat. I took a deep breath, and then another deep breath before I crept ahead. The coals were so hot it was hard to breathe, and I knew better than to linger.

Eventually, I made it to the wall where the cellar door was. Things must have shifted even since Joan was there because the door wouldn't budge at first, and I finally had to give it a hard jerk to get it open, praying I didn't bring the whole house down on top of my head. It didn't quite do that, but I heard enough screeching wood and falling rubble that it had me pretty convinced for a second. But then it subsided again, and I went down the steep steps into what was left of the cellar.

The first thing I found was that part of the ceiling had caved in, crushed by a massive beam of wood which had landed right on the end of the wine rack that held the sweet water. Dozens and dozens of bottles were shattered and spilled all over the floor, beyond hope of saving. I saw at least a few bottles that looked unbroken, but I couldn't tell how many there might be. I didn't dare try to dig them out, either; there was too much broken glass everywhere.

The shelf with the dust bottles had been crushed also, but I couldn't tell how many of those were still whole. Who knew how many hundreds of ex-wolves, lying dead at Andrew Garza's feet before we ever had a chance to wake them. One more horrific crime to lay squarely at his doorstep, but only one among many.

Well. Not good, but it could definitely have been a whole lot worse, I thought to myself. We hadn't quite lost everything, and we could work with that. I crept close enough to snatch an unbroken water jug, and then quickly got back outside, heaving a sigh of relief when I made it back to the lawn. I was drenched in sweat from the heat, and felt light-headed.

"So what's the verdict?" Matthieu asked.

"I can't tell for sure about the wolves. But most of the water bottles are shattered. Not all of them, but I can't tell how much is left; there's too much broken glass to go digging through there with no gloves on," I explained.

"That's not good," Matthieu said, expressing everybody's opinion.

"It could be a lot worse, I guess. We'll have to get somebody out here to tear all this down so we can pull out what's left," I said.

Just then Matthieu's phone rang, and I gathered from the half of the conversation I could hear that it was his mother. I didn't particularly pay much attention, at least not till I heard him say "We'll be right there."

That pricked up my ears, and apparently it did Jolie's too.

"We'll be right there where? And for what?" she asked, and Matthieu lifted up one finger to tell her to wait a minute. It always annoys me when people do that, but under the circumstances there wasn't much we could do except wait. Before long he laid his phone down.

"Orem wants to cut a deal," he said without preamble.

"What kind of a deal?" Jolie asked warily, speaking for all of us.

"I'm not sure. He called Mama and asked her to have us come see him at the jailhouse. He said he'd make it worth our time," Matthieu said.

"I think he's lying," I said.

"Yeah, probably, but I'm sure he knows Andrew and Gabe are still loose and we'd probably be interested in squeezing out whatever information we can get hold of. I told you none of them has a shred of honor," Matt pointed out.

"You mean you really think we should go see him?" I asked.

"Can't do any harm except maybe waste some time. Might as well see what he's got to say," Matthieu said.

So that's what we did. As soon as we got to Natchitoches, we dropped off the others at John and Sarah's place and I rode with Matthieu to the jailhouse to see what Orem had to say for himself. There was supposed to be a rule about not allowing visitors to speak to inmates except by phone through a glass wall, but apparently the Doucets had enough clout to get that waived when they thought it was necessary. When we got there, the jailer took us to a private room with a table, which I guess was supposed to be for lawyers to meet with their clients. Then they went to fetch Orem.

"Remember, he's liable to say whatever he thinks we want to hear. We can't trust him for a second," Matthieu muttered while we waited.

A minute later they brought him in, and he was an ugly mug, I have to say that much. It had been too dark in the guesthouse to see him very well, but under the glare of the fluorescent lights I had no such problem. He had short black hair and narrow eyes that looked shifty and cold, like a snake. Or like the eyes of a man who's done terrible things and isn't the least bit sorry for them. He didn't look very old, though; no more than thirty at the most.

"What do you want, Orem?" Matthieu began, without any pretense of pleasantness. This was business, pure and simple.

"I want out of here, that's what," he said.

"So? People in Arizona want ice water, too," Matthieu said.

"I know you can get me out if you want to," he insisted, looking directly at Matthieu and ignoring the comment.

"Maybe I can. Why should I try?" Matt asked.

"Because I've got some information you'd like to have. I'm willing to trade," he said. Ah, that was it, I thought, nodding to myself.

"What kind of information?" Matthieu asked.

"I keep that to myself, till I know whether you're willing to deal or not," he said.

"I can't say. How am I supposed to know whether it's worth it, unless I know what I'm trading for?" Matt asked. Orem looked at us with barely concealed dislike, but I guess he must have realized we were the ones with the upper hand at the moment.

"All right. Fair enough. I'll tell you what I know, and then I'll leave it up to you to decide whether you think it's worth it to let me out," he said, his shoulders sagging.

"Fine. If I think it's worth it, I'll see what I can do about getting you out," Matthieu agreed.

"You mean you'd really let this scumbag out, after what he did?" I asked, too shocked to remember to keep my mouth shut. Orem gave me a baleful glare, but Matthieu just shook his head.

"Orem is a small-time crook. He's not a werewolf anymore, and all he ever did was sniff along behind Andrew and do whatever he was told. He can't even do magic. Letting him loose doesn't worry me too much. He'll end up back in jail over something else soon enough, anyway," he said, waving it off like it wasn't important.

"Mighty kind words, Master Doucet," Orem said sourly.

"The truth can sting sometimes, I'm afraid. If I'm wrong then I'll be the first one to shake your hand and be glad for you. But in the meantime, speak up and tell me whatever you wanted to tell me, and then we'll see about what happens next," Matthieu said.

"Fine. Andrew's been working on some things, out there at the lab. I don't know what, exactly; I don't understand all that stuff he does. But I know he kept saying if he could get it to work, that he'd own the world someday," he said.

"What kind of a something?" Matthieu asked.

"I told you, I don't know. It's some kind of machine, though. He never would say much about it. But I know he thought it was the most important thing he ever worked on," Orem said.

"It didn't have to do with the zombies?" Matthieu asked, frowning.

"Nope. He said all that was small potatoes, just a way to get some money and a few soldiers, that's all," he said.

"So how come I never heard about any of this before? We watched y'all for months, you know. Seems to me we should've got a whiff about some big mysterious project going on," Matthieu said.

"Andrew's smarter than you think, rich boy. He had a lot going on," Orem said.

"We didn't find anything at the house," Matthieu pointed out.

"No, you wouldn't have. The lab is there on campus in Las Cruces. You wouldn't have thought anything of it, just watching him go to work at the university," Orem said.

"All right, I see your point," Matthieu agreed grudgingly.

"So did I earn my get out of jail free card?" Orem asked sarcastically.

"I'm not sure yet. We'll go check on what you said, and if it turns out you're right then yeah, I'll go say something to the district attorney. Might take a few days, though," Matthieu said.

"All right, then," Orem agreed. He didn't seem happy, but then what did he expect? It was too easy to make up a convincing lie. I knew Matthieu would keep his word if it turned out Orem was telling the truth, but it would have been stupid to believe him without checking it out.

"So what do we do now, head for New Mexico?" I asked when we got back outside.

"Yeah, might as well. If Dr. Garza really does have some big mysterious project going on out there, then we need to make sure it gets nixed while there's still time, before he has a chance to start it back up again," Matt said.

"You don't think the university would have gotten rid of it by now, since he's been gone so long?" I asked.

"Maybe. But I doubt it, if they think he might be coming back someday. We sent them a letter after we nabbed him, supposedly from him, saying he had a family emergency and he'd have to be gone for a while. To cut down on any worries about his disappearance, you know. So I'm willing to bet they've still got all his stuff out there. All we can do is go look and see, though," Matthieu shrugged.

All five of us ended up going, on the theory that it was safer that way in case anything unexpected happened. We went armed to the teeth, too, just in case Dr. Garza *did* happen to be lurking somewhere out there on his old stomping grounds. But I dearly hoped we could run in and out of there quietly and there wouldn't be any trouble.

I'd never been farther west than Fort Worth, and I soon discovered that I hadn't missed much. After twelve hours of being cooped up in a car with pretty much nothing to look at but West Texas scrubland for most of the way, well, you tend to get antsy and bored and people start rubbing you the wrong way, no matter how much you like them. It was hot, too, and even the air conditioner couldn't cool it down enough to be comfortable.

For those of you who have never been to Texas, I probably ought to explain something. About half our state is dry, like you see on westerns and such. The other half is wet and muggy and heavily wooded, just about like anywhere else in the Deep South. And separating these two very different worlds, there's usually a divider called the Marfa Line, sharp as a knife's edge. It's a divider of air masses, not necessarily vegetation, so you can't see it on the ground or anything, but believe me, you will most certainly know when you've crossed it, especially in the summer. If you're driving east, you'll suddenly break out in sweat and feel like somebody just wrapped you in a warm, wet glove. And if you're headed west, you'll suddenly dry out and feel cooler. It fluctuates back and forth, but nine times out of ten you'll cross it somewhere between Dallas and Lubbock. On this particularly fine day, we cracked it right before we got to Abilene, and I've never been so glad to see it.

But still, by the time we got to Las Cruces we were all cramped, crabby, and exhausted in spite of the fact that we hadn't done anything but sit still all day long. I couldn't help noticing the fact that Cameron and Joan were holding hands in the back seat, but I'd already told him what I thought about that. If he wanted to go ahead anyway, then all I could do was hope things turned out for the best.

It was nearly eight o'clock by the time we got there, and the university would have been mostly closed by then even if we'd been inclined to go out there right away, which we most certainly weren't. We stayed at the Ramada Palms de Las Cruces, which had the advantage of being close enough to the university that we could walk there in the morning.

Which is what we did, as soon as we finished eating breakfast. It was unusually cool outside, or so it seemed to me, but maybe that was because of being in the desert. The campus had a vaguely Spanish-southwestern look, but we weren't there to admire the architecture. We had business to do.

It didn't take long for us to find out where Dr. Garza's office was, but locating his lab space turned out to be a whole 'nother thing. Nobody seemed to know, or if they did then they weren't telling.

There was a neat little name plate beside the man's office door, but the place was locked and it was dark inside. I don't doubt Matthieu could have picked the lock to get us inside if necessary, but of course he couldn't do that with people all around.

"Why don't you go ask one of the other faculty members, Zach?" Matthieu suggested, and I raised an eyebrow at him.

"Why should I be the one to ask them?" I asked, not liking the idea.

"Because you've got that corn-fed all-American boy kind of aura, you know; more than any of the rest of us do. You're likable that way. So you're the one they're most likely to trust and help," Matthieu said, and I really couldn't help myself; I busted out laughing.

"Are you serious?" I asked. I'd never heard somebody say such a thing in my entire life and I wasn't quite sure what to make of it.

"Yeah, seriously. You think it's funny but trust me, it matters," he said, without the slightest hint that he was joking.

"But I don't know anything about physics," I objected. True, I've picked up a smattering of chemistry and geology from listing to Justin and Eileen over the years, but not enough to make me look knowledgeable in front of a professor.

"You know as much as any of the rest of us do. But hopefully you won't have to know anything. If he wants to get technical then sidetrack him," he said.

"Fine. Not sure what I'll say, but we'll see," I agreed.

Chapter Six

The only person I found in his office that early in the morning was an older man with salt and pepper hair who looked like he hadn't slept enough the night before.

"Can I help you?" the man asked, when I showed up in the doorway.

"Yes, sir, I think so. I'm thinking about coming to school here next year, and I wanted to talk to you about the physics program," I began. It seemed like my best shot at getting some information.

"Sure. Come on in and have a seat. Do you know what branch of physics you're most interested in?" the man began, and I groaned inwardly. Out of my depth and over my head already, and the conversation had just begun. I wanted to say some choice words to Matthieu for volunteering me for this mission. But there was nothing for it now, so I groped in my mind for something to say.

"Particle physics, I think," I said. The only reason I said it was because I'd seen a program on TV about that subject several months ago, so I hoped I wouldn't seem hopelessly lost if he asked me a question.

"Hmm. . . that's not really my specialty. I do astronomy and space science, mostly. Particle physics is more Dr. Witten's thing, but he'll be in later this morning if you'd like to talk to him instead. But in the meantime I can tell you a little bit about the program and give you some literature," he offered.

"What about Dr. Garza?" I asked, and the man looked at me oddly.

"Dr. Garza does high-energy theoretical work, mostly, but I'm afraid he's not available right now," he said.

"Oh? How come?" I asked, like I didn't already know.

"Well, he unexpectedly disappeared last year, to tell you the truth. Nobody's quite sure what happened to him," the man said, frowning, and that worried me. I was afraid of asking too many questions about a missing faculty member; people start to get curious about why you're so curious, if you know what I mean.

I decided it was time to set him at ease.

"That's a shame. I talked to him for a little while last year when my class came out here for a college day, and he really impressed me," I said smoothly, and the man chuckled.

"Young man, I don't mean to sound harsh, but honestly, why are you really here?" the man asked, looking at me with amusement. Uh-oh.

"What do you mean?" I asked, trying my hardest to give off some of those corn-fed Boy Scout vibes that Matthieu claimed I had.

"Andrew Garza hated students, and he certainly never impressed one. Brilliant he might have been, but nobody liked him, ever. So tell me what's up, and I might even help you," he said.

I hate it when I get caught red-handed like that. The man had seen through me like a glass window, all because I didn't know what I was talking about. But what could I tell him? That Dr. Garza was a werewolf who roamed the Llano killing people and that he practiced sorcery when he wasn't doing physics?

Somehow I didn't think that would go over well. But I was unnerved, and I couldn't think of any other way to explain myself.

"I don't think you'd believe me if I told you, sir. It's a long story. All I can say is that I'm interested in his work, that's all," I finally said.

"Well. . . fair enough. I don't see any harm in telling you that much. It's public information anyway. Like I said before, Dr. Garza mostly worked with high-energy particle physics and theoretical things. Tachyons were a particular interest of his, if I recall correctly," the man said.

"Tachyons?" I asked.

"Particles that travel faster than light. Purely hypothetical, of course, but I know Andrew was supposedly working on an apparatus to detect and possibly manipulate them, among other things. I think he was interested in gravity research, too. If I'm not mistaken, that's what he worked on out there at White Sands," the man said.

"Can you show me his lab?" I asked eagerly, forgetting to bite my tongue before I overstepped my bounds. It was cheeky, maybe, but I was just about out of ideas at that point. But maybe I do have an air of wholesome likeability after all, because the man only chuckled again.

"Sure, why not? Come on," he said, getting up from his desk and grabbing a wad of keys on a ring. He led me down the hall to a door that looked pretty much like every other door in the place, and unlocked it for us. Then he went inside and switched on the lights.

I don't know what I expected to see in there; some kind of sinister-looking contraption that might destroy the world if I pushed the wrong button, maybe. But in reality, there wasn't much in there at all. Some dusty electronics, a few tools, a computer, and on a table in the corner a steel box with a padlock on it.

"What's in there?" I asked, pointing toward the box.

"I'm not sure. Probably Andrew's amazing tachyon detector, if I had to guess," he said, with a touch of scorn in his voice. There was no way I could fiddle with anything with one of the professors standing there beside me. He might dislike Dr. Garza, but there were probably limits to how far he was willing to go.

"Done looking?" he finally asked.

"Sure, I guess," I admitted, acting crestfallen.

He locked the door behind us, but he didn't go back down the hall. He just stood there, playing with his keys and looking at me.

"So now tell me, what's your interest in all this?" he said, and I knew I had to tell him *something.* So I made up the best story I could think of.

"Dr. Garza was a bad man. He worked with my dad out at White Sands, and my dad disappeared last year, too. I think Dr. Garza had something to do with it, so I'm just trying to find out as much as I can," I said. There was maybe a grain of truth to all that, and the implied accusation was enough to sidetrack the professor.

"Oh, I don't think so. Andrew may have been a foul-tempered lout, but I don't think he'd ever do anything *criminal,"* the man said, sounding shocked. I wanted to shake my head at how thick people could be sometimes. If this man only knew.

"Well, maybe not. But I had to check. Nobody else seems to be doing anything about it," I said, letting some fake bitterness creep into my voice.

"I'm sorry for your loss. I hope your father turns up safe and sound, and Andrew too, for that matter," he said.

"Me too. Thanks for talking to me," I said, offering him my hand. He shook it, and then I scooted out of there as fast as I could reasonably get away. The others were waiting for me on a bench outside.

"So what's the deal?" Matthieu asked as soon as I got within earshot.

"I'll tell you in a minute. But for now let's get away from here so nobody sees us," I said.

We went back to the hotel, and once we were behind closed doors I finally felt like it was safe to talk.

"Did you find out anything?" Matthieu asked.

"Yeah, but I nearly got busted, too. That man I talked to said Dr. Garza was doing research on tachyons, and he showed me his lab. I didn't see anything particularly bad-looking in there, but I couldn't snoop around too much with him watching me, either," I explained.

"We'll go back tonight when nobody's there," Matthieu said.

"Do you think that's safe?" I asked, imagining what might happen if we got caught.

"Of course not, but I don't mean super late. That's asking for trouble. The best time to go is in the evening when the building is still open, but the professors and students are mostly all gone home. That way nobody will think it's unusual for us to be there if they *do* see us, but it's not likely that anybody will," he explained.

It made sense, but I thought to myself that I was becoming a real expert at breaking and entering nowadays. Mild-mannered honor student by day, intrepid cat burglar by night, and weekend monster-slayer to top it all off. I smiled faintly.

We went back to the physics building about nine o'clock, an hour before it was supposed to close for the night. Matthieu seemed to be right; the place was deserted except for an occasional student working late. We all stood in front of Dr. Garza's lab door, pretending to socialize but in reality shielding Matthieu from view while he picked the lock to let us in. We all had backpacks on, partly to make us look like students and partly so we'd have something to stuff our swag in.

As soon as we got inside, we stuffed paper towels along the bottom and edges of the door so nobody would see light coming from inside. There were no windows, so we didn't have to worry about that. Then we ransacked the place. There didn't seem to be anything worth messing with at first, but then Matthieu cut the padlock off the box.

In there we found books full of lab notes which we quickly stuffed into our backpacks without bothering to read them yet, along with a small device which reminded me of a cross between an ancient cell phone and a video game controller, if you can imagine such a thing. We took everything that looked even remotely interesting, and I even snatched the hard drive from the computer. Finally there was nothing left.

"Okay, I think we're done, here," Matthieu said in a low voice, and we got out of there quicker than a cat could blink its eyes. I don't think anybody noticed.

We'd already decided not to stay in Las Cruces a single minute longer than we had to, just in case. We drove as far as Sweetwater, Texas, before we absolutely crashed from exhaustion, but at least we were several hundred miles from enemy territory by then.

On the long ride we pulled out some of the lab manuals and tried to make out what Andrew Garza thought he was up to, but it was all Greek to me. The only thing I gleaned from the manuals was that the little controller-type thing was called a tachometer, just like the things you see in sports cars. Apparently Dr. Garza actually had a sense of humor, hard as that was to believe.

The books were mostly dense and complicated math, which is part of why they didn't tell us much. Other parts of them were obviously written in code, no doubt to keep nosy thieves from reading them. Still, you can get a hazy kind of idea of what's going on in an equation if you know what all the symbols and variables mean, just like you can get a hazy idea of what a newspaper article is about even if you only understand one out of every three words. So we methodically looked up the symbols online, trying to get a feel for things.

We did find out one interesting little tidbit. The tachometer was built to handle some incredible amounts of energy. I mean like thousands-of-nuclear-bombs-type levels of energy. At first we thought maybe it *was* some kind of super bomb; that would fit with Dr. Garza's personality, all right. But then I spotted a symbol that said the equation was endothermic; that is, it absorbed that much energy, instead of giving it off. So, no bomb, then.

"What kind of reaction would need that much energy to make it happen?" I wondered out loud, but nobody had any idea.

"It's a shame we don't know any physicists," Cameron muttered.

"I bet we could find one. There are plenty of colleges around," Matthieu said.

"Yeah, that's true. Just going in to ask what some equations and lab notes mean probably wouldn't make anybody suspicious," I agreed.

Thus it was that we ended up making a detour to visit the University of Texas at Arlington, to show our books to one of the physics faculty there. I was drafted for the job of going inside again, but I didn't mind so much this time since we didn't have anything to hide. The agreed-upon story was for me to say that the books belonged to my recently-deceased uncle, who was wealthy and a bit eccentric.

I found a faculty member who was willing to take a look, finally. I didn't know quite what to expect, but I have to say that what I heard was probably the last thing I would have expected.

He thumbed through the book carelessly for a few minutes, and finally laughed.

"Yeah, your uncle was definitely eccentric, that's for sure," he said.

"So what does it mean?" I asked.

"Well, among other things, it looks like he was trying to build a machine to control gravity, to intensify it within a given area by weakening it elsewhere, or vice versa. Looks like it would work, on paper at least, but I'd have to see it to believe it. But then he goes on to say that if you intensify the gravitational field beyond a certain point, and if you've got enough energy, that you could control the time stream, too. That is, if you didn't end up destroying the planet in the process, which he seems to imply might be the case. So I'm not sure if it would really do you any good," he said.

"So you mean he built a time machine?" I asked, and that seemed to amuse the man even more.

"There's no such thing as time travel, son. At least not the way you think. You couldn't go back and visit your grandpa when he was a boy or anything dumb like you see in movies. It violates the law of conservation of energy, plus a dozen other natural laws. What your uncle seems to be saying is that you could freeze time inside a small bubble, while the rest of the world goes on normally. I *might* go along with that. But reverse time, or jump backwards? Not in a million years. If it worked, something like this might give you a one-way trip to the future, but even if you got there then you'd never make it back. But now *here* he's talking about tachyons, and how he could detect them so he could see what's going on in the future. Now *that* might be useful," he said thoughtfully.

"But I thought you just said. . . " I said.

"Yeah, I know I said you could never go backwards, but like most things there's an exception to every rule. See, time is a funny thing. The faster you move, the slower time passes. It's a measurable effect, even at fairly slow speeds. You can start out with two perfectly synchronized watches, and if one of them is moving rapidly, say in a bullet train, while the other one is sitting still, it won't be long before the moving watch falls behind the one which is at rest. Simple enough, right?" he asked.

"Yeah, I guess so," I admitted.

"Well, okay, the faster you go the slower time moves, until eventually you reach a point where it completely stops passing.

That happens at exactly the speed of light. Now, if you could go faster than light, then, theoretically at least, time would reverse and start passing backward. But nothing can go faster than light because of one other little rule. Besides slowing down time, speed also increases your mass. So the faster you go, the more mass you've got, and therefore the more energy it takes to make you go even faster. So, there comes a point when your mass would be infinite, and therefore it would take an infinite amount of energy to make you go any faster, which is impossible. Want to guess what that point is?" he asked.

"Um. . . speed of light?" I guessed.

"Bingo. That's why we call it the speed of light barrier. There's not enough energy in the entire universe to cross it, unless you've got no mass at all, like light. But some people say there might be particles which have *always* traveled faster than light, and in that case they wouldn't *need* to cross the barrier, you see. Those are tachyons. Nobody's ever actually found one to prove they exist, but if they did then it's possible they also travel backwards in time just like we travel forward, and if you could catch them just right, then you might be able to get some information about the future they came from. Now, like I said, I don't believe it for a second, but it's at least possible, I guess," he said.

"But how would you get a machine like that to work?" I wondered out loud, and the man just stared at me.

"I don't believe it's possible to build anything like that in the first place, but even if it were, then you'd have to talk to whoever built it to figure out what the controls mean. Same way two different brands of computers might do the same job, but they don't operate quite the same way," he said.

"I see," I said. My head was spinning from the crash course in theoretical physics, but I didn't know what else to say. A time machine that only worked in one direction was kind of a let-down, in a way. Whenever you think about things like that, you always think about visiting the past, or if you do think about going ahead, you usually imagine coming back home at some point. This machine was a one-way ticket to the future, with no chance of ever coming back, and what good was that?

Then it crossed my mind that, combined with the tachyon detector, it might be pretty useful, indeed. You could look ahead and see who won the Kentucky Derby next year, and then if you were a betting man you could probably make a ton of money. Or if you were a criminal, you could always escape into the future where the law could never touch you. If you were smart and unethical, there were all kinds of possibilities for riches and power, I suppose. But cleaning up on lotto tickets or getting away with bank robbery didn't seem like all that enchanting of a use for a tool like that, at least not to me.

There was a show on TV that I used to like, about a man who always got the next day's paper from the future and then he had a chance to save peoples' lives if there was going to be a house fire or a train derailment or whatever it was. I remember thinking how utterly cool that would be, if it could really happen. Now it seemed that maybe it actually had, although not exactly in the way I'd always imagined it.

But my puzzler was puzzled out for the moment.

"Thanks a lot, Dr. Eberly. I understand everything a lot better, now," I said.

"Sure, no problem," he said, and that was the end of it.

Chapter Seven

"We need to take all this stuff somewhere Dr. Garza won't think to look for it. We can't let it fall back into his hands again," I mentioned as we were leaving the university.

"What difference would that make? He can always build another machine, since he built the first one," Jolie pointed out.

"No, Zach's right. I'm sure Dr. Garza could build another machine eventually, but we don't want to make it easy for him in the meantime. He'll have a hard time re-creating all these lab notes and data sets, and that's good. We want to delay him as long as possible. And besides that, if he gets the tachometer back then *we* won't have it," Matthieu reminded her.

"Yeah, but the problem is, he seems to be really good at tracking us, when he wants to be. I'm not sure there's anywhere we can go that he won't know about sooner or later," Cameron said.

That was a depressing thought, but there was no way anybody could argue with it. Dr. Garza had found us in Red Lick the very first night, and he hadn't had any problems pinpointing us at the hospital, either. I don't know if he had a crystal ball or if he was just diabolically smart and lucky, but either way he was an excellent tracker.

We ended up going to a random motel on the north side of Tyler, hoping it might keep us hidden for a day or so until we could figure out what to do. We couldn't keep on staying in motels forever, moving from place to place like nomads. But the problem of how to fight back against Dr. Garza's sorcery was a tough nut to crack.

If we'd still had the rings, then things might have been different. We could've turned the monster back into dust and been done with him. But unfortunately that wasn't an option anymore, not after crushing them into dust on top of Mont Mouchet last fall.

Well, I guess I should clarify that. We only crushed the jewels, not the bands, and Celine Doucet had replaced the gems with new ones so they looked exactly the same as they always had before. We even still wore them occasionally, but they were powerless now, heirlooms and symbols of office but nothing more. I had one myself now, and so did Cameron. When Angie and Sarah retired back in April, we both accepted the offer to take their places. So then Rob Doucet anointed us with oil and we swore a solemn oath to fight evil wherever we might find it, to the utmost of our power, before he gave us each our ring. It was all very formal and ceremonious. We weren't Werewolf Hunters anymore, either; we were Avengers. A new name for a new and broader purpose, they said.

Thus it was that I became only the fourteenth holder of the Ring of Barthélemy since 1769, and that was something I took seriously. All six rings were named after the one who first wore them, and mine had belonged to Barthélemy Chrétien from 1769 until 1790, when he was killed in battle against radicals during the French Revolution. Cameron had Barthélemy's brother Sebastién's ring, which I always thought was a cool coincidence.

But sadly, even though an ancient ceremonial ring may be an impressive thing to have and to wear, I was under no delusions that it would impress Dr. Garza at all.

I plugged in the hard drive to Matthieu's laptop to see if there was anything useful on there, but there didn't seem to be. Just more physics stuff which none of us understood and copies of final exams and things like that.

On the other hand, we did find out a few personal things about Dr. Garza. We soon discovered that he had all kinds of plans for mayhem. Bombs, mostly; he really did seem to be fond of those. But he seemed to like tormenting individuals and families even more, when he got the chance. He was smart enough to write his notes like they were nothing but made-up stories, but I never doubted for a second that every bit of what we read was true. He seemed to have a special hatred for people who did good things, especially in the future. It was sad reading.

No, he wasn't responsible for all the sorrow and heartache in the world, not by a long shot. But he sure did do his part to add to it, I've got to give him that. He also had a list of names and addresses with no explanation as to why, and that was puzzling. The only guess we could come up with was that they were potential victims he might be thinking about.

"Maybe I should warn some of those folks to keep their eyes open," Matthieu muttered.

The tachometer was what really interested us the most, though, so before long we gave up on the other items and gathered round the table to see what it could do. We took it out of the case, and then Matthieu gingerly pushed the power button.

Well, it didn't explode, at least. All it did was bring up a command screen full of boxes asking for a precise date, year, and time. Pretty self-explanatory, surprisingly. And then above it, seemingly floating in midair, was a black and white globe where you could zoom in on the location you wanted by using your finger as a mouse. I have to admit, that part impressed me more than anything else I'd seen so far. Oh, I knew it was just a trick with holograms and probably not even that hard to do, but what can I say?

Matthieu typed in a date for six thirty in the evening a week in the future, and then zoomed in on Dallas because that was easy to find. Soon a grainy black-and-white image of a supermarket parking lot enveloped us like a bubble, and if it hadn't been for that cheap-surveillance-camera video effect, it would have felt just like we were standing there. We could look in any direction and see what was happening.

"This is awesome," Cameron said, speaking for all of us.

"There's nothing to show us what the date is, though," Matthieu frowned.

"See how close you can get. I see a newspaper rack over there by the door, I think," Jolie suggested.

The illusion of being at the store was so real I forgot myself and started walking toward the doors, only to find myself stepping right through the image and back out into the motel room.

That was jarring, to say the least, and when I turned around all I could see was a silvery sphere about ten feet across. It looked solid from the outside, but it wasn't. My finger went right through when I poked it, so I took a deep breath and stepped back inside, never feeling a thing. It was more or less like a mini-planetarium, I guess.

"Enjoy your trip?" Cam asked, grinning.

In the meantime Matthieu had figured out how to shift the view closer to the building, using the controls on the machine. We soon got close enough to tell that it was indeed a newspaper rack, but that's when we discovered a serious limitation. The closer we got the blurrier it became. There was no chance of reading a future newspaper or anything like that, and we soon discovered another major drawback. We couldn't see indoors unless it was through an open door or a window. We were perpetually stuck outside, and there was no sound, either. It was like watching a silent, black-and-white movie in full 3-D, odd as that sounds.

"How can we tell if we're looking at next week or not? It's too grainy to see the newspaper," I complained.

"Scroll down the street and see if we can find a bank clock or something like that," Jolie said.

Matthieu quickly did so, until he came to a bank which displayed the date, time, and temperature on a big screen by the sidewalk. We all waited with anticipation for the display to switch over. Sure enough, when it did, it read 6:49 pm, on the date he'd specified.

It was so cool to think we were watching the future that we kept staring at it for a long time after that. Even watching cars roll down the street was fascinating, knowing it wouldn't actually happen till next week. There were fits of static now and then for no apparent reason, but other than that it was easy to watch.

I was amazed Matthieu and Jolie ever managed to catch Dr. Garza by surprise out there in New Mexico, if he had a machine like this. But then, I don't guess he had time to watch the tachometer constantly; he did have a job, and he did have to sleep now and then. I really don't know.

But eventually the attraction of watching people pump gas and walk down the street in the future started to pale a little.

"Should we try the time control function?" Matthieu asked, his finger above the button.

"Sure, why not? Just don't set it too far ahead," I said.

"I'll set it for ten minutes from now," he said, punching in the date and time just like he had with the viewer. The silver bubble popped back into existence around us, only this time it was blank and featureless.

"That'll work," I agreed.

"Oh, hey, this is new," Matthieu said.

"What is it?" I asked.

"It's asking me to choose a power supply," Matthieu said.

"What do you mean?" I asked.

"It says grid, enth, or mass," Matthieu said.

"What's enth?" Jolie asked, interrupting the conversation.

"No idea. I'm sure it's an abbreviation for something else, but I couldn't tell you what. I'm not a physicist," Matthieu said.

"Try grid," I suggested, and he shrugged.

"Ready?" he asked, holding his finger above the EXECUTE button. It seemed like a vaguely sinister word to use, even though I knew it was common enough.

"Go for it," I said, and he punched the button.

Two things happened at that moment. The first one was that the tachometer disappeared, along with the silver bubble around us, and the second thing was that the lights went out.

"Hey, what happened?" Matthieu said.

We found ourselves in a dark room, and it was several minutes before the lights came back on. I found out later that we'd blacked- or browned-out all or most of ten different states for almost twenty minutes with our little test-drive. That's what you get, when you don't know what you're doing. You tend not to think that pushing a button on a little machine will end up making headlines in a dozen major newspapers the next morning, but there you go. The tachometer was lying on the floor, just where it would have been if Matthieu had dropped it.

"I guess now we know what grid means," Cameron laughed.

"Yeah, but did it work?" Jolie asked.

I checked my watch, and compared it to the clock on the wall. The clock was battery powered, and it was exactly ten minutes ahead of my watch. I guess a jump of ten minutes into the future doesn't amount to much, but I can't deny it was awesome. It would have been awesome to travel through time even if it had only been for ten *seconds,* and for a moment, even though he was a fiend in so many ways, I saluted Andrew Garza for his brilliance.

"What's the deal with the tachometer? I know I didn't drop it," Matthieu said.

"Maybe it stayed put when it sent us forward, and then since your hand disappeared it fell to the floor. Then it stayed there for ten minutes till we popped back in again, and there it was," I said. I'd been thinking about it, and I was pretty sure that was what happened. I don't know *why* it happened like that or why the tachometer itself seemed to be immune to time-jumps, but then of course I didn't build the thing.

"Should we try it again, maybe a little longer this time?" Matthieu asked.

I was tempted; we all were, I could see it on their faces. But if it worked like everything else, then the longer the jump the more energy it would take, and we'd already caused enough disruption just for a jump of ten minutes.

"I don't know about that. We don't want to suck the electric company dry again," I said.

"What if we switched it to one of the other power sources?" Jolie suggested.

"Well. . . we still don't know what enth means, and I'm not too keen to find out the hard way," Matthieu said.

"Mass probably means mass conversion. That creates a lot of energy, so it ought not take too much," Jolie said.

Matthieu switched it to mass conversion and started to set the controls, but then I guess he must have thought better of it.

"You know, maybe we ought to put off another test drive for a while, after all. I know it's cool, but we really don't know what we're doing with this thing, and we already saw what can happen. Maybe we better wait till we find out more," he said.

I thought about that, and reluctantly decided maybe he had a point. Sometimes discretion is the better part of valor. We had the lab books to study, so maybe with some hard work and study we might find ourselves in a better position to use the tachometer safely.

We decided after a lot of thought to go back to Natchitoches. Sarah Doucet's house was the closest thing to a fortress that we had, and since apparently we couldn't hope to hide from Andrew for very long, the next best thing was to fortify our position.

I think Dr. Garza must have had other plans.

I'm not sure how he found us again, unless he actually did have a crystal ball or something similar. There might have been some way for him to trace where all that power was going during the blackout, too; he was probably smart enough to figure out something like that if he needed to. But however that might be, I was woken up at three o'clock in the morning to the sound of the motel room door being blown off its hinges.

All of us were instantly awake, like you might imagine. The first thing I saw when my eyes cleared was Andrew Garza coming through the blown-off door with a ball of white-hot fire in his hand. It reminded me of a comic book I saw once, with a character who could throw fireballs from his hands like baseballs. More sorcery, no doubt, and I rolled off the bed in a tangle of sheets just in time to miss getting fried. The mattress went up in a cloud of acrid smoke, and before I knew what was happening the sprinklers came on. Getting woken up in the middle of the night to fight a homicidal maniac in a dark hotel room in the pouring rain is one of those experiences I really don't wish on anybody. For a while, everything was fire and water and shouting and chaos.

Then, all of a sudden, there was a sonic *boom* so loud it shattered the windows and almost deafened me, and when I came to my senses I realized Dr. Garza was gone, and there was a smoking, red-hot crater in the floor almost ten feet wide and three feet deep. It was smooth as silk and perfect all the way around, and I surmised that it must have been a sphere to start with, because part of the bed was gone, and so was a good-sized chunk of the bathroom wall.

The room was full of smoke from the fireballs and the crater, and the carpet was still on fire in several spots in spite of the sprinklers.

"Let's get out of here!" I yelled, praying the tachometer wasn't ruined from getting drenched. Somehow it had slid down to the bottom of the crater, and Matthieu was already down there grabbing it. That was enough for me; I didn't wait to see what happened next. We didn't want to encounter any curious guests by using the front door, so we climbed out the smashed window instead, shell-shocked and soaking wet. It gave me flashbacks to the explosion at Miss Edith's house, even though it was nowhere near as bad as that had been.

In all the confusion, none of us realized till we gathered up in the parking lot that Joan wasn't with us.

"Where's Joan?" Cameron asked, and nobody had a clue.

"Where's *Dr. Garza?* And what *happened* in there?" Jolie asked. Two more excellent questions for which nobody had any answers.

"Joan must have used the tachometer to drag Dr. Garza into the future," Matthieu said, and as soon as he uttered the words, none of us doubted for a second that that was exactly what Joan had done.

It had been a brave thing, and she'd almost certainly saved our lives by doing it. But now she was lost somewhere in time, with Dr. Garza right beside her. They might pop back into real-time at any minute, or they might not show up for centuries. The tachometer was soaking wet and wouldn't even come on, so there was no way of knowing what time it had been set for.

"We've got to get out of here, *now.* The cops and the fire department will be here before you know it, and we can't let them get hold of the tachometer. If they want an explanation about why we ran out of here so fast then we can think of one later," Matthieu said, interrupting my train of thought.

He was right, of course, and even though I didn't like the idea of leaving Joan there with no help if she *did* come back, I yanked open the car door and got inside. Joan had already proved several times that she was no weakling, and I had to trust that she could handle things on her own.

As soon as we were all loaded up, Matthieu left the parking lot so fast you'd think he was born to be a race-car driver, and fifteen minutes later we were out of Tyler and out of reach of any curious authorities, at least for a little while.

"I don't know how she did it. She didn't even know how the thing worked," Jolie said, shaking her head.

"She watched Matthieu, just like all of us did. It wasn't that complicated. Obviously she knew enough, and she probably thought it was the only solution to keep us all from getting incinerated," I said.

"She was probably right. She saw the writing on the wall and she knew the game was up if she didn't do something drastic. She was a soldier, remember? She's used to having to make tough calls like that. Dr. Garza had us trapped in that room and he would've burned us all to ashes, if she hadn't done what she did. That's what we get, for letting him catch us off guard again," Matthieu said.

"We'll have to start looking for her as soon as we can; she'll have to show up sometime," Cameron said.

I remembered all too well what Dr. Eberly had said about how there's no coming back, and in my heart of hearts I hoped the tachometer hadn't been set too far ahead. It wasn't just the fact that Joan had already saved our lives twice by then, although that was part of it. It was also the fact that I knew what it would do to Cameron if she vanished completely.

"I don't see any way to do that, except to watch the motel constantly till she shows back up. That could take forever," Jolie said.

"No it won't. I'll skip ahead fifteen minutes at a time, just long enough to see if she's there or not. Then I'll keep going till I find her," Cam said.

"You might, if that thing still works. It got pretty soaked back there," Matthieu said, and Cam's face fell.

"All we can do is hope," he finally said.

We drove as far as Shreveport, an hour away and safely out of the state. Well, honestly I don't know how *safe* it was; nowhere felt particularly safe right then, but it was one less worry, at least. It was almost too late to be worth going back to bed at that hour, but not quite. Matthieu rented us another motel and we collapsed for what was left of the night.

When morning came, we sat glumly around the room trying not to think too much about Joan and what might have happened to her (or was going to happen, or however you wanted to say it). The tachometer was more or less dried out by then, but I had my doubts about whether we could get it to work or not. Moisture and electronics don't mix very well. But there was nothing to do except try it, so that's what we did.

We never could get it to come on.

"That's what I was afraid of," Matthieu muttered.

"We'll keep it, see if it dries out better in a few days. You never know," Jolie said. I knew she was saying it mostly for Cameron's benefit, but we all had good reason to hope the tachometer started working again. If not, then Dr. Garza might pop back into real-time at any moment and catch us completely by surprise again, and we all knew we might not survive a third such attack. That machine was our only warning.

But there was nothing to be done about that except pray, since the tachometer was one-of-a-kind and the only person on earth who might've known how to fix it was also the last person on earth we wanted to run in to.

We got back to Natchitoches quietly, and took all the stuff from the lab down to the basement at Matthieu's house, including the dead tachometer. That was as safe a place as we could hope to find.

Chapter Eight

That same afternoon, we all got together on the patio to talk about what to do. Or at least me and Jolie and Matthieu did. Cam mostly just sat there and listened, still preoccupied with Joan, I guess.

"The real problem is that we don't have any defense against the Garzas' magic. Andrew is too strong for us, especially without the rings. We saw that in the motel last night. It's only a matter of time before he gets back and nails all of us," Matthieu said.

"That's a cheerful thought," I said.

"Cheerful or not, it's the truth. We've got to find some way to neutralize his sorcery or we're dead meat. Gabe too, for that matter. That whole family is a menace," Matthieu said.

"Didn't you say they had a sister, too?" I asked.

"Yeah, Layla. But she's not much of a problem unless you kiss her," he said.

"Kiss her?" I asked.

"He means that's the only kind of magic she does. If she kisses you then she'll take your life away and make you turn old. That and disguising herself is all she can do. So as long as you keep your lips to yourself, you don't have to worry about *her,*" Jolie interrupted, putting a possessive hand on my arm. I wanted to laugh, but of course I didn't.

"Well. . . I guess we could look in the history books; they might give us some ideas, at least. We can use the concordance, see if there are any references to sorcery in there," Matthieu said.

It was the only idea anybody could think of, so we adjourned to the dining room to follow up on it.

There are books everywhere in Sarah Doucet's house, most of them old and dusty ones with leather covers. Some had titles in French or Latin and a few of them are bigger than a Bible in a church. They're stacked and crammed into every available shelf, table, and surface, in no particular order that I've ever been able to tell. The house is beautifully furnished with all the usual modern things in other respects, but the books make it feel like some musty library in a castle in Transylvania. The fact that a large percentage of them are devoted to werewolves only reinforces that impression.

"Who *wrote* all these books?" I asked as we went down the hall.

"Oh, various people. A lot of them are by family members, writing down case histories. You never know when something one person learned might turn out to be useful again. Others we got from libraries or from pod members or things like that. I'm not sure if we'll find anything, though; it's mostly all wolf stuff. Even the Garzas started out like a normal werewolf case, till we found out everything else about them," Matthieu said, and in spite of all my dealings with them in the past, it still sounded odd to be talking about a "normal" werewolf case. It seemed like a contradiction in terms.

"I'm sure they did," I agreed dryly.

"They really did. But people surprise you sometimes, Zach; that's why you've got to be ready for anything, even when you think it's only your typical run of the mill assignment. The

Garzas were only my third case, honestly. Uncle Rob assigned it to me because we all thought at first it would turn out to be an easy one, just sweep in one afternoon and nail them, you know. Good practice for me and not too dangerous. So I went out there and cased the joint, and that's when I saw the zombie on the back porch. That put a whole new light on things in a hurry. I didn't even know what it was, when I saw it the first time. And then somehow Dr. Garza must have found out I was spying on him, because he came outside and looked right at me where I was hid in the rocks. Then I swear he threw a bolt of white fire at me, or something like that, just like he did at the motel last night. I barely had time to drop to the ground and run before he fried me. I fired a couple rounds to let him know I was armed, and maybe that stopped him from chasing me; I don't know. I'm pretty sure he could've caught me if he'd wanted to. Wolves are fast like that, even on two legs. I had a magazine full of silver bullets if I needed them, but even that won't always save you in a close fight. I had to run almost a mile and a half back to the truck and then I got out of there in a hurry, believe me," Matthieu said.

I always like listening to Matthieu and Jolie's battle stories. They make things sound so glamorous and exciting. But then on the other hand I can't help remembering that even though danger is exciting, it's also dangerous. I'm not such a thrill-seeker that I feel the need to go looking for trouble if I don't have to. It finds me on its own quite frequently enough, it seems.

"So what happened then? How'd you catch him?" I asked.

"You can read the story sometime if you want to. I wrote it all down in the case notes," he said, and with that I had to be content.

He went on to talk about the finer points of semi-automatic pistols and how he personally preferred the Glock .45 when dealing with wolves and how he spent three to five hours a week at the firing range to sharpen his aim. I listened to all this with a healthy respect; I always thought I knew something about guns, but Matthieu could have taught a class on the subject.

By then we'd made it to the dining room, where we all sat down around the big mahogany table while Matthieu used the concordance to look up some books for us to read. The concordance is actually a computerized reference system to help locate information, and I hadn't even known that it existed until recently. Matthieu printed a list of books with references to magic or sorcery, and then handed me one of them to start reading.

It turned out to be a history of werewolf activity in Switzerland, a topic which was interesting enough if only for its strangeness, but there was no time for idle curiosity. Somewhere in those pages was a reference to magic of some kind, and it was my job to find it. So I skimmed, and after a while came across a passing reference to the fact that a certain lady werewolf named Henrietta Maldorf in the village of Grindelwald had possessed an item called a Guardian Stone in 1879, which, apparently, made it impossible to capture her. She was unfortunately killed in battle with the werewolf hunters, and she'd apparently tossed her Stone into a crevasse rather than let it fall into the hands of her enemies. That was all the book said about the subject.

It sounded promising, so I used the concordance myself to look up what a Guardian Stone might be. There were only fifteen books in the library which mentioned that topic, so I figured it shouldn't take too long to check those out.

It's a shame the library itself isn't organized as well as the concordance, but it's not. Finding the name of a title you want is easy, but actually locating where it is in the house is a whole 'nother story. Matthieu and his parents usually know where everything is, but I don't see how anybody else ever would. The book I wanted was called *Days of Yore,* and Matthieu had to fetch it for me from a shelf in the third-floor hallway.

It turned out to be a history of Saint Madryn of Gwent, whoever that was. She seemed to be an awfully interesting and colorful sort of person, after I read about her for a while. Eldest daughter of Vortimer the Blessed, Queen of Gwent after his death, and a devout evangelist who preached the gospel all over

Wales and Cornwall and southwest England around the year 500 A.D. She was a sworn enemy of the pagan Druids who still existed in the land at that time, and apparently several of them had attacked her with curses and spells. But her faith in God was such that all these attacks came to nothing, and more and more people listened to the gospel.

Near the end of her life, Madryn feared for her people lest they fall back into sin and error for fear of the magic of the Druids. So it was said that she acquired three stones of the kind known as Cornish Diamonds, of exceptional purity and brilliance, and these she blessed such that they might guide and protect her most devoted followers. These stones she gave to the ones she deemed most in need of them, and in time her dearest wish came to pass, and Britain became a Christian kingdom. So said the book.

It went on to say that no magic could affect the holder of a Guardian Stone, and they gave to their owner true dreams, to show him which way God would have him go. But they were also holy, and anyone of evil intent who touched one bare-handed would be scorched and burned by it.

"I think this might be what we need," I said aloud, tapping the book with my finger. Then I told the others what I'd read.

"Oh, yeah, I remember those things, now that you mention it," Matthieu agreed.

"Really? How come y'all never went after them, then?" I asked.

"Well, we never really needed them for anything, Zach. There are a lot of things in the world we could've spent our time looking for, if we'd wanted to. It's like asking why we never went looking for buried treasure or the Fountain of Youth. We never had a good enough reason to want to," he said.

"Not even when you found out Dr. Garza was a sorcerer?" I asked.

"No, because we still had the rings back then. That was good enough," he said.

"True, but that was then, Matt. We *don't* have the rings anymore, and it seems like one of the Guardian Stones would be the perfect thing to have *now,*" Jolie said, and he frowned, thinking about it.

"Maybe so, if we can find one of them," he finally said.

"That other book I was reading at first said one of them is in a crevasse in the Grindelwald Glacier, in Switzerland," I said.

"Might as well scratch that, then. We could spend a hundred years looking for that one and still not find it. Even if it hasn't been crushed to powder by now, that is," Jolie said.

"Well. . . there are still two more," I said, trying to be optimistic.

This called for a refocusing of our research priorities, but even after a diligent search, what we came up with wasn't much.

"Here's something, I think," Matthieu finally said.

"What is it?" Jolie asked, putting down her own book.

"One of them was last seen in the possession of a Spanish captain by the name of Juan de Velasco, commander of the warship *San Andrés* on the Pacific coast of Mexico. Looks like he was a fairly big dog back in the day; a navy admiral and the nephew of the Viceroy of Peru. It says here he was caught in a hurricane in August or September of 1600 and driven far north and west before his ship finally sank within sight of land off Cape Mendocino, in California. The wreck is four miles south of the cape, in three hundred feet of water at the edge of an undersea canyon," Matthieu said.

"How come it hasn't been salvaged, then?" I asked. People will do almost anything to find sunken treasure.

"Well, probably because it's a warship and there's nothing down there worth messing with. Except possibly the Guardian Stone, of course, and nobody would know or care about that except us," he said.

It sounded pretty good, until we started doing a little bit of research about Cape Mendocino. Turns out that's a pretty forbidding place to make any kind of dive. There are strong currents, and the water is dangerously cold, let alone the fact that three hundred feet is almost twice as deep as you're supposed to go unless you're a highly experienced diver, which me and Cam certainly weren't. People have died doing stupid things like that, and not so very rarely, either.

But in spite of all our searching, we never found the faintest clue as to where the third Stone might be. The last recorded sighting of it was in Virginia in 1689, and after that it seemed to have dropped off the face of the earth for all we could tell.

"Well, folks, it looks like we've got a choice between the glacier and the ocean. Take your pick," Jolie finally said.

"Now I see why nobody ever bothered with these stupid things," Matthieu muttered.

"Seems like it's not much of a choice to me. If the glacier is hopeless then California is the only other option," I said.

"We don't even know for sure if that's where the Stone is, though," Matthieu said.

"All we can do is try. It's either that or get burnt to a crisp by Dr. Garza whenever he gets back," I said. Nobody could argue with that, so Matthieu finally sighed.

"Well. . . I guess it could be worse. So happens I know how to dive, but I can't go down there by myself. At least one other person will have to go with me. If y'all work really hard at it, you could probably finish your classes and get certified in a few weeks, though," he said.

"You know all kinds of things, don't you, Matt?" I asked dryly. I really didn't mean for it to sound snarky, but Matthieu is so good at so many different things he makes me feel like I'm incompetent sometimes. He pretended not to notice.

"Anything that might keep me alive during a mission. You never know what might turn out useful," he said.

"You think it's safe to wait that long? I mean, not knowing when Dr. Garza might show up again, or what Gabe might be doing in the meantime?" I asked, and Matt shrugged.

"It'll have to be. No way am I going down there with a couple of newbies who never even went snorkeling before. It's too dangerous," he said firmly.

I wanted to tell him I'd been snorkeling lots of times, but I kept my mouth shut. I knew what he was talking about.

"Well, me and Cam really need to go home for a while, Matt; we've both got work and baseball practice and things like that we need to do. Is there anywhere around Texarkana where we can take the classes?" I asked.

"Give me a few days and let me look around. I'll find something," Matthieu said.

We drove home not long after that, and found that Justin had been pretty busy himself while the two of us had been otherwise occupied for the past few days. He'd called in some people with heavy equipment to pull down what was left of Miss Edith's house, and by the time we got back home the work was done. The second we found out it was safe, we immediately went out to Red Lick to salvage whatever we could from the wreckage.

"Not much left," I said, staring at the bare ground. There was nothing left on the lot except a few scraps of wood and glass, and a big hole in the ground where the cellar used to be.

It made me sad, although I'm sure if Miss Edith had been there herself, she probably would've told me not to value sticks and stones too much, or something similar. She always did like to bring everything down to brass tacks that way.

We walked over to what was left of the groundwork and found that the cellar steps were still in place. The heavy beam that crushed the shelves was still down there, too, and the place was still full of broken glass and nail-studded pieces of wood. But even with all that, I spied an unbroken bottle sitting on the bottom of one of the shelves.

"See that?" I asked, pointing to the bottle.

"Yeah. I guess we better go down there and see what we can salvage," Cam said. We had some tough leather gloves so we wouldn't cut our hands, and several empty plastic containers just in case we found any broken bottles that weren't completely empty.

We ended up saving twenty-three bottles of sweet water, when all was said and done. Nineteen originals, plus four more we refilled from what was left in the broken ones. Twenty-three, out of all those hundreds. It was a thousand times better than nothing, but still, it seemed like such an awful loss.

But even worse were the wolves. We found not quite five hundred of them still intact. I didn't want to do the math to figure out exactly how many were shattered, but I knew it had to be well over a thousand. The thought of it made me sick.

"Do you think we've got enough water for the rest of them?" Cameron asked, looking at the bottles skeptically.

"I hope so. Maybe. There are four hundred and eighty seven of them left. That works out to about one bottle for every twenty wolves. Not sure. It'll be tight," I admitted.

"I wonder if there are any more like the Garzas in there? We might not *want* to wake up all of them," he said.

"Matthieu and Jolie always said there were a few really nasty ones. I guess we'll have to look through the files, see who survived and try to pick the ones that we think deserve a second chance the most and start with them. Then we'll help as many as we can. It won't be easy to choose," I said.

"No, it won't," he agreed. I didn't look forward to that job at all, but after the debacle with the Garzas I was a firm believer in showing extreme caution. I'd seen how easily things could get out of hand.

"I did find one thing down there we might want to hold on to. For when Joan comes back, you know," I said, pulling a bottle from my pocket. The label said *Annabelle Rusk, December 23, 1864.*

Cam didn't move at first, and then slowly took Annabelle's bottle from my hand. I hoped if I let him hold on to it that he might feel a little better.

"I thought it might be better to wait for Joan to get back before we wake up Annabelle, so they'll still be the same age, you know. We better set aside a little bit of water for her, just to make sure we've got some left when the time comes," I went on, handing him an empty but unbroken dust bottle. He quietly filled it up with water from one of the jugs, and then put it in his pocket along with Annabelle's dust.

It was several days before Matthieu was able to find a good place for us to take our scuba classes. There are not too many spots in this neck of the woods where you can get any practice for a really deep dive like the one in California would be. The deepest lake within a thousand miles is less than two hundred feet deep, and even the Gulf is shallow for a long way out. You have to go nearly eighty miles offshore from Galveston to find water the same depth as the *San Andrés* was wrecked in. That made things difficult.

We finally had to settle for Lake DeGray, which is about an hour's drive north of where we live, in the foothills of the mountains. It's warm and blue and crystal clear, studded with rocky islands and not too crowded. But not too deep, either. It's only about 180 feet deep at the most, but that turned out to be the best we could hope for.

So we took our classes in Arkadelphia, and Matthieu rented a motel room for a month so he could stay there and coach us all afternoon on the days when we didn't have something else we had to do instead. Jolie took the classes too, and I guess we sort of made it a hobby, you know. We would have been swimming a lot in the evenings all summer anyway, so diving wasn't so very different.

Things settled into a semi-normal routine after a while, even with the uncertainty of what might happen with the Garzas. Me and Cam made pretty good money working for Jeb Barling, and we practiced hard for our baseball games; enough that we both won all-star medals. We were the best students our dive instructor ever had, and spent so much time in the lake that I started to think we might grow fins.

But even with all those hours on the ranch and the playing field and in the classroom and in the water, I think Cam still had too much time on his hands. He went mudding with Jake and Levi once or twice, and he'd sit up reading till all hours of the night. But his heart wasn't in any of those things, like it would have been only a few weeks ago. The summer that started out looking so bright and enjoyable for both of us had turned into a barren wasteland for him, it seemed, no matter how busy he was.

He did play with Joey a lot, and sometimes both of them would doze off on the couch in mid-afternoon, Cam with his mouth hung open as usual and Jo-jo asleep on his chest. He rarely socialized much with the rest of us, though.

I think if Joan had died or he knew for certain that he'd never see her again, then it might have been easier. But as it was, there was always that tiny thread of hope; and he was hanging himself with it.

Chapter Nine

"I've been acting pretty dumb lately, haven't I?" he finally asked one night while we were lying on our beds, and I knew immediately that he was talking about Joan.

"You want to tell me about it?" I asked casually. I could have said *I told you so* or something similar, and I don't know but what he wouldn't have agreed with me. But that would have been cruel, and I wanted to make him feel better, not worse.

"What is there to tell? She's gone," he said. He was staring at the ceiling with his hands crossed behind his head, looking like somebody had tried to cut his heart out with a rusty knife.

"I'm sorry, bubba," I said.

"Yeah, me too. To tell you the truth, I don't know what I would've done or how things would have worked out, if she hadn't disappeared. Maybe it never would've amounted to anything, anyway. I just don't know. I'm sure it's all for the best, when I can put aside my feelings and think logically. But that's hard to do, you know," he said.

"I know," I said.

"Did I ever tell you how my father died?" he asked. He never had, actually, and it didn't seem to have a whole lot to do with what we'd been talking about, but I was willing to listen to whatever he felt like saying.

"No, you never did," I said.

"He got kicked in the head by a horse. He went to bed with a headache that night and then never woke up," he said.

"I'm sorry," I said again.

"We lived in Black Springs then, on my grandpa's ranch. You remember the deer camp? That's part of it, or at least it used to be. But Mama didn't get along with anybody after Daddy died, so we moved away. After that I never spent longer than a few months in one school or one house till I came here. I never had a chance to make any friends or get used to anything except bouncing around like a tumbleweed all the time. It was awful," he said.

"Yeah," I sympathized.

"I remember drifting from town to town, sleeping in Mama's Blazer sometimes when we didn't have anywhere else to go, living off free lunches at school and whatever we could scrounge from leftovers at restaurants and suchlike," he said.

I felt a wave of pity for him then. I know what it's like to have nowhere to go and have precious little to live on but hope. If you think stuff like that never happens in the real world, then you've lived a sheltered life and you should thank God for your blessings.

"I never knew that," I said.

"Oh, it wasn't *always* that bad; Mama had a job sometimes, and then we usually had a house and all the normal things. But she kept getting in trouble for killing cows and fighting with people, and then we'd always have to drop everything and run somewhere else. I've lived everywhere from Florida to Missouri and West Virginia to Texas and just about everywhere in between, at some point or other. I feel like. . . I don't know. . .

every time I start to get close to anything, it gets ripped away from me," he went on.

That was really the crux of the matter, of course. When you grow up like that, you tend to develop a hard knot of fear in your heart, an almost incurable idea that love can't be trusted and the world is a cruel place where you don't dare let your guard down. It's hard to get over it, and if you *do* by chance open up a little, then any kind of loss hurts ten times as much as it should have. That was Cameron's worst trouble with Joan, I think. Losing her was like rubbing rough-grit sandpaper all over a spot which was already sore from other things, and that's why it broke his heart the way it did.

But self-pity will lead you into bitterness if you're not careful, and sometimes sympathy will only make it worse. There are times when what you really need most is for somebody to tell you to get a grip and think about something else for a change. Justin has always had a real knack for knowing when those times are, but even I could tell that this was a time when Cameron needed it.

"Don't, Cam," I said.

"Don't what?' he asked.

"Don't be bitter. Remember who you are and what you believe," I said.

He looked at me for a minute, and then gave me a crooked little smile.

"That's exactly what Justin told me," he said.

"Yeah, but it's still true," I said, and he sighed.

"I know, Zach. Really I do. Sooner or later I'll even act like it, I promise. No worries," he said.

"Okay, then. But *I'm* not going anywhere, though. Just so you know," I said staunchly, and he laughed a little.

"No, I guess not. You and Justin and Eileen have already been around longer than anybody else I can remember," he agreed, and that was that.

We all went down to Galveston for three days toward the end of June for a test dive in the Gulf; the closest thing to reality that we could hope to find before the real thing. Matthieu chartered a boat so we could go far enough offshore to find some deep water, and things went pretty smoothly in spite of my qualms. Of course I knew the warm, placid Gulf wasn't much more like the California coast than the warm, placid lake had been, but I tried not to think too much about that.

We tried to have some fun while we were there, too, if only to take our minds off what lay ahead. We rented bikes to ride along the seawall, and went to the amusement park out on the Pleasure Pier, and fished for spotted seatrout and red drum at Seawolf Park. I like Galveston, even if it's a bit touristy sometimes. It's a colorful mélange of saltwater taffy and sharktooth necklaces, barefoot beachcombers and sand all over everything. I don't get to go down there very often, but when I do it's always fun.

But even amidst the playing, I can't deny that I still found my eyes drifting out more than once across the blue-green ocean, and thinking about what was to come.

On the third day, Matthieu booked us a flight from Houston to Eureka, California for the very next morning, with a layover in Salt Lake City. We got there that same evening in time to rent an SUV and gather all the equipment we'd need the next day, and to get a good night's rest before we tackled the ocean. We had a bottle of sweet water with us, just in case of emergencies, but we all knew that wouldn't save us if something went wrong out there under the water.

I guess Matthieu knew what he was doing, though. He asked a lot of questions at the dive shop and ended up getting three wetsuits and some scuba gear with rebreathers and tanks full of oxy-helium instead of plain air. Not to mention waterproof GPS gear, sharp knives in holsters, and other things. The knives looked ominous, but when I asked him what they were for he gave me a long look before answering.

"Just in case," he finally said, which didn't make me feel any better at all.

"Just in case of what?" I asked.

"There are a lot of sharks in this area. Great Whites. The big man-eating kind. A knife won't help much if you get attacked but it's a lot better than nothing. Also in case you get tangled up somewhere and have to cut yourself free," he said.

"Zach, if you get killed by a shark I swear I'll jump in there and beat it to death with a rock if I have to," Jolie said, and I laughed a little.

"Don't worry, babe. No shark's gonna eat me, I promise. I'd give it indigestion for a week," I said. Everybody knew that was mostly bravado, but hey, it sounded good.

But whatever our private hopes and fears might have been, we left early the next morning for Cape Mendocino, determined to have done with it all. Matthieu drove us along a steep and winding road so narrow and deserted that I hesitate even to call it a highway, and after about forty miles or so we finally reached the Cape itself.

It was a beautiful sight; I have to say that much. There were little black rocks speckled in a turquoise sea, and a huge island of solid stone reared up right offshore. You could see it all really well from the hilltops. But the wreck site wasn't quite at the Cape, so we followed the road along the coast for a couple more miles until it bent back inland.

"Okay, folks. This is as far as we can drive. We'll have to walk it from here," Matthieu said.

We all got out, and from there we had to walk down the beach for another mile or so before Matthieu called a halt and pointed out to sea.

"Right out there, a little less than two miles, is the edge of the canyon. It ought to take us about two hours to reach it. Then we'll head west along the edge till we come to the wreck, which shouldn't be that far. We'll grab the Stone, hopefully, and then head directly back here. If anybody gets lost, head due east and you'll get to shore pretty quickly. The water is cold and you probably won't be able to see more than twenty or thirty feet at the most, so stay close together. Take it easy and don't exert yourselves or you could pass out and drown. We've got around six to eight hours of air, depending on how fast we use it. Keep an eye on your gauges. This won't be a walk in the park," he said.

We quietly put on our gear, in no mood for joking around, and when everything was ready we all held hands in a circle while Matthieu prayed for safety. I spent a few minutes talking quietly to Jolie, and then kissed her one last time before slipping my mask on. Then we waded out into the choppy water. I had an icy lump of fear in my gut, but sometimes you have to be face-brave even when you can't be heart-brave. There was nothing to do except keep a cool head and pray one more time that we came home safe.

We could still see the Cape Mendocino Rock in the distance, prominent against the sky. It was beautiful, but it seemed sinister, too. I wondered how many sailors besides Juan de Velasco had gazed on that rock with their last sight before they drowned in the cold Pacific, and I shivered.

The water wasn't quite as frigid as I feared it would be, maybe because the wetsuit kept me warmer than normal. But it was cold enough to make me shiver when we first got in, and it was worse after we got completely under the surface. There were a lot of sand particles stirred up in the water near the beach, but it did clear up a little bit as we got farther out from shore.

We had to pass through a kelp forest at one point, thick and green and easy to get lost in if we hadn't had our GPS devices. We saw lots of fish and several sea lions, and maybe I would have noticed more things like that if I hadn't been so ill at ease. I kept thinking about sharks, and I couldn't help but notice how far away the surface was. The pressure builds up really fast as you keep getting deeper; it takes more effort to breathe, and the light starts to fade out and turn blue. It's an awfully alien world down there, right on our own doorstep.

We had radios built into our helmets, but we didn't talk much. Partly to save breath and partly because I wasn't the only one who was edgy. Me and Cam sat up late to watch *Jaws* last summer on *Macabre Theatre*, and now I dearly wished we hadn't. Those are images you definitely don't want to have dancing in your head when you're deep under water and can't see more than ten feet in front of your face. I kept imagining an open mouth full of teeth suddenly appearing out of the murk, and had to force myself not to think that way.

That said, the trip down to the canyon was mostly just tedious. About two hours after we left the beach, we were roughly three hundred feet deep according to our depth gauges, and that's when we came to a sudden drop-off.

I'm sure it would have been an awesome sight, if the water had been clear enough. If the maps were right, then that cliff dropped well over a thousand feet into inky blackness and the south rim was nearly two miles away. All I could do was imagine it, though, because visibility was still pretty bad. We could see maybe thirty feet at that point.

Matthieu didn't waste time admiring the nonexistent view, though. As soon as he saw that we'd reached the drop-off, he stopped.

"West," he said, clipping his speech as short as possible. The helium in his breathing mix made his voice sound high-pitched and strange, almost like a cartoon character, but nobody was in the slightest mood to laugh.

We picked our way west along the rim of the canyon, which was fairly straight in that area. I thanked God for that small blessing; if we'd had to follow a convoluted edge then it would have taken much longer, and I was already starting to feel the cold seeping into my very bones, in spite of the wetsuit.

After about thirty minutes of following the canyon we spotted her.

The *San Andrés* was lying yawed slightly to one side, half buried in sand. Her masts were nothing but stumps, and there were several holes in her sides where wood had rotted away, I guess. If she'd been a treasure ship then I might have been tempted to explore the hold and see if there was any gold left inside, and I might have drowned my stupid self in a momentary fit of greed. Gold fever is very real, if you don't watch yourself. But we all knew there was nothing valuable on board, and in spite of some mild disappointment I knew that was probably for the best.

But still, she was a real, honest-to-goodness Spanish galleon, and that by itself was something worth seeing. The Captain's cabin was up at the rear of the poop deck, which thankfully was one of the easier places to reach. With a little luck, we'd find the Stone and be back on shore in another two hours.

Things didn't work out quite that way.

The three of us were passing by one of those big holes in the hull when a tentacle shot out and wrapped itself around Matthieu, followed almost instantly by others. I saw one of them grab Cameron, and before I even had time to react a third one seized my right leg. All three of us were yanked inside that black hole faster than you could blink an eye.

In the confusion and shouting and strobe-like effect of flashlights being flailed around and dropped, I caught a glimpse of the hugest octopus I've ever seen or imagined. I don't know what it was doing there, unless maybe it had decided the *San Andrés* was its own personal cliff-side condo, even better than a cave. But whatever it thought about that, it clearly intended to have us for lunch. It was already trying to fasten its sharp beak on Matthieu's ribs.

And there was *nothing* I could do about it. The thing still had me gripped in one of its strong arms, and another arm was slithering around my midsection. Within seconds I'd be pinned with my arms held down against my sides, if I didn't think of something fast.

I watched a show last year about the most dangerous and extreme sports in the world, and it so happens that one of them is called octopus wrestling. People dive into the ocean from a pier, come to grips with a giant octopus, and then try to manhandle it out onto the beach. Sometimes they manage to drag it out of the water and barbecue it for their friends, and sometimes the octopus holds them under till they drown. It's a popular pastime in Oregon and Washington, or at least according to the show it was. I remember thinking at the time that you'd have to be grade-A certified crazy to take up a "sport" like that.

Now here I was, locked into a wrestling match with a monster who was stronger than all three of us put together.

I remembered my knife, and somehow I managed to get it out of the sheath attached to my weight belt. Then I started hacking at the tentacles that seemed to be all around me. It's hard to do anything very effective in the dark, against an enemy with eight slithering arms. And I guess octopuses are not stupid, either. He might not have understood what a knife was, but he knew full well which one of us was hurting him. Soon I felt more tentacles enfolding me, and then an agonizing pain as he bit me on the side, right below my ribs. That sharp beak cut right through my wetsuit and it felt like he took a chunk out of me, too.

I kept stabbing him with my knife but it didn't seem to be doing any good, and if I'd been alone then I think it might have ended in disaster. But then all of a sudden he disentangled himself and shot a cloud of ink into the water so thick that it wiped out what little light there was in the first place from the dropped flashlights.

"Zach, are you all right?" somebody yelled in my radio, and I couldn't tell if it was Matthieu or Cameron because of the distortion from the helium.

"I'm fine, but he *bit* me!" I yelled back.

I touched somebody's moving arm, and we grabbed hold of each other.

"Whose hand is that?" I asked, forcing myself to calm down and stop breathing so hard.

"It's Cam. Where's Matt?" he asked. Matthieu hadn't said a word during all this, and that alarmed me.

"Matt, where are you? Answer me!" I said.

Silence, which filled me with dread. The ink was still too thick to see anything, so all we could do was feel around in the dark and keep calling him. He never answered, but finally my hand touched something that felt like neoprene.

"I found him," I said.

Matthieu still had his flashlight clipped to his belt, and I switched it on. We could see just enough to make it back outside, and once we were out of the ink cloud I saw several bite marks on his wetsuit, and blood slowly seeping out into the water.

This was *not* good.

"You're bleeding, too," Cameron said, looking at me. My side was throbbing from the bite, and I guess bleeding, too, but I couldn't help that right then.

"We've got to get him back to shore," I said.

"Go get the crystal first. I don't want to have to come back down here again. I'll wait here with Matt. Just hurry!" Cam said.

"What if that thing comes back?" I asked.

"Well, yeah, I guess I better come with you," he admitted.

Thankfully, people don't weigh much under water. We dragged Matthieu away from the octopus's lair, up onto the main deck of the ship. The Captain's cabin was right behind there.

I was in considerable pain, and light-headed from carbon dioxide build-up during the fight. That's exactly why Matthieu told us not to exert ourselves too much during the dive; it can make you pass out, and if that happens then you're probably a goner. That might have been what happened to him, for all I knew. I *hoped* that was all it was.

One thing was certain. I had to calm down and take it easy, or I *would* pass out. So I made my way slowly into the cabin at the back of the ship, taking Matthieu's flashlight with me to light the way.

There wasn't much to see back there when I reached the cabin. What was left of a table and chairs, a bed, and a desk. A crucifix nailed to the wall, and on the floor beneath it the skeleton of a man holding a set of rosary beads in one hand. Presumably Juan de Velasco, the Captain himself.

But all that was secondary, because I caught a glint of light as I swept the flashlight across his other hand. When I directed the beam there, I saw a clear crystal the size and shape of a peach pit, clutched tight in his bony fingers as if it were the most precious thing he possessed. If even half the things I'd heard were true, I guess it probably was.

I wasted no more time. With a respectful nod at the skeleton, I quickly swam over there and pried his fist open. The bones had been in that position for so long they broke when I tried to move them, but I hoped Captain Velasco would forgive me for the necessity. I snatched the Guardian Stone from its long resting place, shoving it inside the zippered pocket on my belt. Then I got out of there, leaving the dead in peace.

"Did you get it?" Cameron asked as soon as I got back outside.

"Yeah, I got it. Come on," I said.

Chapter Ten

We headed back, but that was a lot harder than the trip down there had been. Matthieu wasn't heavy, but it was cumbersome to pull him along and slowed us down. I was still hurting pretty bad from the bite, and still bleeding, too, and so was Matt. Everybody knows that fresh blood in an area known to be infested with sharks is a bad idea; they can smell it from miles away and it drives them crazy. We kept looking over our shoulders nervously, even though the water was too murky to see anything until it was right on top of us anyway. I hadn't forgotten about the octopus, either. He might decide to come back and finish us off. I've heard that octopuses in captivity are famous for holding grudges against certain people; this one had more reason to want payback than one of the captive ones ever did, and better opportunity to get it, too.

I felt a little bit safer when we passed through the kelp forest, since it gave us some cover. But it also slowed us down even more. I was exhausted from the long swim, and chilled to the bone from that ice-cold water, and my muscles were starting to get stiff and hard to move. That happens, if you stay down in cold water for too long. It's a danger sign that you need to get out immediately. I knew that, and I knew if you *don't* get out soon then you're liable to die from hypothermia even if you don't drown first. But there was nothing to do except keep plugging along, praying we made it out before it was too late.

We stayed near the bottom to make ourselves less conspicuous since sharks like to attack from below, but that was our only defense. Thank God, we never saw one.

We switched over to a fifty-fifty oxygen-nitrogen breathing mix when we got shallow enough, to help decompress faster. That last hour of swimming is probably one of the hardest things I've ever had to do in my life. The extra oxygen helped, but my arms and legs were numb by the time we struggled to our feet in the surf. The wind and the waves were brutal by then, knocking us down in the water several times before we finally crawled up onto the rocky beach.

I pulled my helmet off and lay there on the ground groaning, wondering if I'd ever have the energy to get up again. We didn't come to shore in the same place we left, but that was only to be expected. We were much farther north, back toward the Cape.

But we still had to walk to the car, however far that turned out to be, and I couldn't imagine walking another ten feet to save my life, let alone having to carry Matthieu.

"I'll go get Jolie if you can stay here with Matt," Cameron said.

"Yeah, I guess you better. Are you okay?" I asked.

"Better than you are. Stay right here and I'll be back as soon as I can," he said.

He shucked off his air tank and most of his gear, leaving it in a pile on the beach, and then trudged off in his wetsuit toward the car as fast as he could. It wasn't too fast, but it was better than I could have done at the time. I watched him for a long time, till he finally disappeared around a rocky outcrop.

Matthieu was still unconscious, but he seemed to be breathing normally at least. So I sat with him and watched the foamy waves crash the shore, and hoped I never had to go on another adventure like that as long as I lived. They make great stories if you're sitting around a campfire laughing with your friends a few years later and comparing battle scars, but at the time they're not fun at all.

It must not have been all that far to the SUV, because before long Jolie showed up, driving down the beach to where we were. I suspect that was highly illegal, but at the time I couldn't have cared less about things like that.

She must have been afraid of the hypothermia and the bites, because she immediately gave me a sip of sweet water as soon as she got out of the car. It didn't get rid of the exhaustion or the cold, of course, but I let out a long sigh of relief as the octopus bite faded away. Matthieu needed it worse than I did, but we couldn't give him any till he woke up. It took all of us together to wrestle him into the back seat, and then we wearily loaded up the equipment.

Then at long last the doors were shut, the heater was on high, and we were on our way back to Eureka.

"What happened down there?" Jolie asked.

"Got in a fight with a humongous octopus that tried to eat us for supper, that's all," I said, making it sound like a joke. It had been anything but, of course, but it sounded so much better to tell the story that way.

"Seriously?" she asked.

"Yeah, seriously. Biggest one I ever saw. We kicked its teeth out, though," I said with satisfaction.

She was quiet for a while, listening to us tell her all about our valiant fight with the giant octopus at the bottom of the sea and everything else that happened down there. But when we finished up with the part about dragging Matthieu ashore covered in bloody bites, she broke in.

"I hope he wakes up soon. We need to get some water down him," she said.

"We might need to have him checked out at the hospital, don't you think? He's been out of it for a long time now," Cameron said.

So that's what we did, and in this case we didn't have to make up any stories. All we had to do was tell the doctor we'd been deep diving at the Cape and got in a fight with an octopus. He could think we were insanely stupid if he wanted to, and probably did, but I'm sure it wasn't the first time he'd ever heard stories about people doing stupid things.

It turned out Matthieu had lost a lot of blood, and he was unconscious partly from that and partly from carbon dioxide poisoning, just like I thought. He also had pretty bad hypothermia. The doctor told us more than once how lucky he was to be alive, and I believed him.

But he finally woke up for a little while early that evening, and Jolie was quick to give him a drink before he slipped away again. Five minutes later he was up on his feet, fine as frog hair, and the doctor was left mutely shaking his head at what a remarkable recovery it was.

* * * * * * *

We flew back to Shreveport instead of Houston this time, and Matthieu took the Guardian Stone to lock it up in his mother's safe in Natchitoches, to keep it safe for whenever it might be needed. Then things reverted to a kind of watchful peace again.

We got home just in time for the biggest ballgame of the summer, against our arch-rival Hot Springs, for the right to play in the state championship. I'd like to say we beat them bloody, but alas, you can't win them all. They topped us by two points in the last inning. So close, but no trophy. So we all shook hands and congratulated them and rooted them on to go win State. If you've got to get kicked in the dirt, then at least you want the team that beat you to be the best one.

That ended our baseball dreams for the year, but I wasn't disappointed, or at least not too much. I had my all-star medal, and there was always next year.

Justin and Eileen surprised us with the news that they wanted to take all of us on a family vacation for two weeks in August, one of those long road trip things to see Yellowstone and maybe some other national parks close by. Road trips are fun when you don't have to fight evil sorcerers or giant octopuses along the way, so I was excited about the idea. They can sometimes be less than fun with a baby along, of course, but Josiah usually went to sleep whenever he was in the car for very long.

Deep down I kind of suspect Justin was thinking it might possibly be our last chance to do something like that together before me and Cam graduated. I'd been around him long enough by then to know how his mind worked. I know some people might have laughed at him for loving us so much, but I never would.

That was right before we got the tachometer working again.

I guess it must have finally dried out to the point that it was able to function. I've had phones like that before, that I thought were ruined and then they ended up being all right after a few weeks. However that may be, all of us were thrilled at the chance to collect some more information.

Matthieu and Jolie brought the machine up to our house, and then the four of us sat down at the kitchen table to see what we could find.

The memory was erased, meaning there was no way for us to know what time the machine had been set on when Joan pushed the button. So we did the next best thing and used Cameron's idea, focusing in on the motel in Tyler and then fast forwarding ahead in fifteen minute increments to make sure we didn't miss it when Joan and Dr. Garza popped back into real-time.

For the first few weeks there were a lot of clean-up activities going on, which was only to be expected, and then the motel reopened and things seemingly went on pretty much as usual. But after hours and hours of flipping through time, we'd looked ahead only about a month, and there was still no sign of Joan or

Dr. Garza. It felt like being on a long-term stake-out waiting for a drug bust, or something like that.

"It looks like this might take awhile," I finally said.

And so it did. One by one, the rest of us got discouraged and quit looking, but not Cameron. He sat at the kitchen table all day, staring at pictures on the tachometer, searching for his lost love. We all knew that's what it was about and why he was so determined, whether he admitted it or not. But love is a beautiful thing, and the whole world bows down in awe at the sight of it, they say. None of us had the heart to tell him to stop.

I did start to worry about him after a few days, though, and I know Justin and Eileen did too. He barely ate, and he stayed up till all hours of the night searching till he couldn't keep his eyes open any longer. He didn't even take a shower unless Eileen told him to. Now and then I'd find him in the morning with his head down, asleep on the kitchen table in front of the tachometer. I couldn't tell how fast he was going or how much time he was able to cover, but apparently he wasn't finding anything.

I heard a phrase once about the "deep deserts of futurity"; I wonder if that writer had any idea of how deep those deserts really are, and how much time there truly is. It was like looking for a single grain of sand out of all the beaches on Earth.

All that was bad enough, but what started to worry me even more was what he might do if he *did* find her. She had to be a considerable distance ahead, if it was taking him this long to find her, and I was more than half afraid he might go off after her without saying a word to anybody, whenever and wherever she might be.

I tried to keep an eye on him after that when I could, but I still didn't tell him to stop looking. That would only have started a fight, and I guess sometimes there are certain things a person just has to work out for himself. I sure hoped he learned his lesson sooner rather than later, though.

And in the meantime, I had other things on my mind, too.

Cam didn't take part, but the rest of us spent the next several weeks waking up wolves right and left, such as were left of them. I think that experience would make a story all by itself. We met some downright strange people in those few weeks, and a few nasty ones. But all of us were gun-shy after the Garzas, even Matthieu and Jolie, and we were a lot more careful than we used to be. We took the people as close to where they came from as we reasonably could, and if they hadn't been asleep too long then we woke them up somewhere near civilization, dressed them, left some money in their pocket, and then high-tailed it out of there before they ever quite came to their senses enough to ask questions. The less they knew about us, the better.

There weren't as many older ones, thankfully. I guess because the werewolf hunters hadn't been as efficient in the old days, and no doubt it had been harder to collect information and to travel back then. Not to mention the fact that the older bottles were mostly glass, and therefore more likely to have shattered in the explosion. But the ones we did have, we stayed with long enough to explain to them something about the modern world and how to survive in it, though we still never gave out our names. I'm sure they had a much harder time than the others, but we did the best we could for them.

A lot of them had lost family or friends in Dr. Garza's explosion, and there was no way for us to explain that; I wish we could have, but what could we have said?

When all was said and done, there were five wolves left that we all agreed it probably wasn't safe to waken, and these Matthieu took back to Natchitoches and locked up in his mother's safe. We had just enough water to finish the job, and when we woke the last wolf then that was the end of it, other than the little bit we set aside for Annabelle. It was a sad moment in some ways, but gratifying in others because I knew that was the purpose it was always meant for. The Hope of the werewolf hunters, finally accomplished in a way that I believe Joram Ross and Miss Edith would have been proud of. To be able to fulfill at long last a promise made centuries ago is a deeply satisfying thing.

Just about the time we finished up with the last of the wolves, Cameron came to me looking pale and miserable, and honestly it hurt me to see him like that.

"I found her," he said, in a dull voice. We were out in the barn that day, and a warm breeze was blowing the clean scent of rain in from the fields. The way he said it sounded ominous, like finding her hadn't been a good thing at all.

"Where is she?" I asked, preparing myself for the worst.

"She's in Mississippi, in 2135. Been there for almost a year already, by the time I found her. I missed them when they first got back. The motel gets demolished in a few years and there's a big warehouse standing there in its place, so I couldn't see inside. But she found a way to get in touch with me, anyway," he began.

"How?" I asked.

"She came back a year later and spray-painted *Joan was here* on the side of that building I told you about, with a time and a date under it that I knew was still several days ahead. So I flipped ahead, and there she was. She walked over to a sand bank and scratched out an address in Biloxi, so I'd know where to find her, I guess. She let it stay for a while, and then she erased it. Five minutes is as good as forever, when you've got a tachometer. Then she looked up like she was trying to tell if I was looking, and I could almost swear she saw me, Zach. She looked right at me," he said.

"Why'd she wait so long to get in touch?" I asked.

"Well, she had to run from Dr. Garza at first, you know. She didn't dare stick around, not knowing where *he* was. So she caught a ride out of town with a truck driver, and that's how she ended up in Biloxi. It took her a while to find a way back to Tyler after that, and she had to survive in the meantime," he said. I didn't know what to say to that, so I waited for more.

"So anyway, I skipped ahead a few days and looked at the place she told me. She had a big sand board on a picnic table out in the back yard, and one day she went out there and wrote me a long story, told me everything that happened. Said she loved me and hoped I'd be okay without her," he said, and took a ragged breath. I didn't know what to say to that, either.

"She's married, Zach," he said, and I could hear the grief in his voice. Cam might be ancient history to her, but for him it was still barely a month since she disappeared, and he'd worn himself down to nothing trying to find her for the past few weeks. One of the cute little side-effects of time travel.

"I'm sorry, bubba," I said, not able to think of anything else.

"She said his name is Philip Carpenter, and he's a good guy and he looks a lot like me. She said it was the only way she could stay legal, since she didn't have the right papers and stuff. It was either get married or get deported, pretty much. Isn't that funny?" he said, his voice thick. The irony was impossible to miss, of course; Joan was probably the oldest living American in 2135, and yet she was in danger of getting locked up and deported for being in the country illegally, all because she couldn't prove who she was.

"I know it's hard," I sympathized.

"No, Zach. You don't know. You really don't," he said.

"You're right, Cam. I don't. Can't pretend I do. But I know what it feels like to lose somebody I love, and you're my best friend. When you get cut then I bleed, too," I told him, and for a second he almost smiled.

"Well, then, you'll be needing a transfusion soon, bro, cause I'm bleeding a lot right now," he said softly.

"I can see that," I told him, wishing there was something I could do to cushion the blow. In my heart of hearts I was kind of glad to hear it, in a way, since it meant I didn't have to worry about him running off after her any more. But I hated to see him hurting so much.

"I'll be all right, sooner or later. Doesn't feel that way, but I know I'll get over it. If Mama ever taught me anything, that'd be it. I guess I should thank her for that," he said moodily.

That was another thing I couldn't think of a good answer for, so I just stood there and waited for him to go on.

"Anyway, I just wanted to tell you, so you wouldn't be worried about me. I know what you've probably been thinking; that I'd use the tachometer to go after her as soon as I found her," he said, and I was surprised he was so perceptive. My first impulse was to deny it and tell him I'd never dreamed he'd do such a thing. But of course that would have been a lie, and even worse, he would have seen through it immediately.

"Yeah, it did worry me a little," I admitted.

"Well, you don't have to, anymore," he said.

"What about Dr. Garza?" I asked.

"I don't know. She said she nailed him in the ribs with that little knife she always keeps strapped to her ankle. She knows how to use a knife pretty well in close quarters; did you know that? They taught her that in the Army," he said. I thought wryly of the letter-opener she grabbed off the cabinet that first day, and resisted the urge to say something about how it didn't surprise me at all.

"Did it kill him?" I asked instead.

"She didn't think so. She didn't stick around to find out; she ran while she had the chance. So I'm sure he's still there, no doubt with some kind of plot going on in his nasty little mind," he said.

I almost suggested using the tachometer to find out, until I remembered it was useless unless you knew exactly when and where to look. Unless we went back and caught him as he left the building so we could follow him, then there was precious little chance of finding Dr. Garza till *he* got good and ready to be found.

"Cam, I really am sorry. I didn't want it to turn out like this," I said, not wanting him to think I was glad. But he only sighed.

"I know, Zach. But it's over and done with now. Nothing left to worry about," he said.

"I'm sorry," I said again.

"Oh, I'll be all right. I always am," he said.

The news that Dr. Garza was banished permanently to the distant future was a huge relief, even though there was no telling what kind of havoc he might cause in *that* time. Or what he might do to Joan if he ever found her, for that matter. He certainly didn't seem the type to forgive anything. There was still Gabe and maybe even Layla to think about, too, even though neither of them had caused us much trouble so far.

But there was nothing to be done about any of *those* issues, at least not immediately, and you tend not to think too much about things you can't do anything about. Besides which, I had plenty of nicer things to look forward to instead. Summer was gradually drawing to an end, and our trip to Yellowstone was coming up, and then senior year with all the stuff that that entailed. My thoughts were full of college applications and baseball scouts and things of that nature, and deep down I was glad of it.

Jolie wanted to go to the main campus of the University of Texas, in Austin, so I was inclined to think that's probably where I'd go, too. I would have liked something a little closer to home, but Austin was near enough that I could still come back and visit anytime I really wanted to.

I wasn't sure about Cameron, though. He never seemed all that interested in college, but I'd heard him talk about building houses with Levi and his dad, or if not that then I knew Jeb Barling had offered him a full time job on the ranch more than once. He likes things like that; working with his hands and doing stuff outside. So if the Rangers didn't call in the meantime, then those were probably the tracks we'd both find ourselves on come next summer.

Whatever happened, I knew we probably wouldn't be seeing each other very much anymore, and that was the one thing that made me kind of sad when I thought about the future, even though we both had so many things to look forward to. I know it's the way things are supposed to be and nobody can stay a kid forever, but I guess in my heart of hearts I never thought it would happen so soon or so fast.

As it turned out, things changed even faster than I thought.

Chapter Eleven

Three days later, Cameron came to me with the most serious look on his face that I've ever seen.

"What's wrong?" I asked immediately.

"It's Dr. Garza," he said without preamble.

"Yeah, what about him?" I asked.

"He found Joan yesterday. Or he will, anyway; I don't know how to say it. But he showed up in Biloxi and killed Philip; burned him completely to ashes," he said.

"I'm sorry, Cam," I said, feeling like I'd said it a thousand times already.

"Yeah, me too. But that's not what I came to tell you about, or at least not mostly. There's somethin' a lot more important than that," he said.

"What is it?" I asked.

"Well, you know how he threw that ball of fire in the motel room?" he asked.

"Yeah, I remember," I said.

"Well, he was fixing to do the same thing to Joan. I saw it in his hand, and he had her backed up against the wall in the living room," he said.

"And then?" I asked, dreading to hear the answer.

"That's the strange part. Then *I* showed up with one of Matt's Glock .45's and nailed him, right through the front door," he said.

"What?!" I cried.

"I know you heard me, Zach," he said. I definitely heard him, all right, and I knew instantly what it meant, too. But that was too much to deal with right away, so, in the way of most all people at all times, I seized on a lesser issue to avoid having to face the main one.

"How come he didn't fry both of you, then?" I asked.

"You got me, there. It's like he wasn't able to, somehow. He turned around and threw the ball of fire at me instead of her, but all it did was splash around me like water. Didn't even singe a hair," he said.

"You must have had the Guardian Stone from the *San Andrés,*" I said.

"Maybe. I don't know all the hows and whys right now. All I know is, I saw myself shoot the man," he said.

"But. . . " I said, and then stopped, not even sure what I wanted to say. Cameron paid me no mind, though.

"Now here's the thing, Zach. If what I saw is really true, then you and me both know what it means. I'm stuck in that time, just like she is. There's no way around it. But the two of us talked it over, I mean Joan and that other me, and then she wrote out on her sand board that the only way to handle things would be for me to take Philip's place. She said the two of us look enough alike that I could pass for him if I have to. Otherwise I'll have the same problem she did, with no papers or anything. I'll have to pretend to be him so I can get a driver's license and all that good stuff. We won't be able to stay in Biloxi because that's where he's from, but we can always go live somewhere else," he said.

I was barely listening to all that, but he was right, as far as it went. There was no coming back from the future, and he was lucky indeed that he had a place he could slip right into, even if he had to pose as a dead boy.

"What about the body?" I asked. That also was really the least of my worries, but I didn't know how to put what I really cared about into words.

"You mean Dr. Garza? Well, he's not got anybody who'll turn him in missing; not that far in the future. I guess we'll take him out after dark and chain him to some cinder blocks and dump him in the Gulf," Cameron said coolly, and I swallowed hard. Sometimes I think he must have read *way* too many true-crime books in his life.

"Cameron, did I ever tell you how cold-blooded you sound, sometimes?" I asked him.

"Well, Zach, honestly. . . what do you want me to say? The man's a stone-cold killer who's tried to whack every single one of us at some point or other. And he *has,* several other people, and he would have done it to me and Joan that day if I hadn't shot him, just like he did to Philip. He got exactly what was coming to him, and you know that," he said, a little severely.

"Yeah, I know. Just never thought I'd be having a serious discussion about how to get rid of a body, that's all," I said weakly, trying to smile.

"Yeah, well. . . just remember it won't happen for a really long time yet," he said, and then I did smile, in a sick kind of way.

"Sounds like you already made up your mind what to do," I said.

"I guess I must have, since I saw myself there. I'm not sure it's even *possible* to change my mind or to do anything different at this point. But even if it was, I couldn't just sit here and watch while he turns her to ashes, could I?" he asked.

"No, you can't do that," I admitted. Leaving Joan to be incinerated by Dr. Garza even when he knew he could save her would make him a hypocrite on so many different levels; a bad Christian, a faithless Avenger, a selfish boyfriend, and basically a sorry excuse for a human being. He couldn't do that, and I couldn't ask him to.

"But there's something else, too," he said.

"More?" I asked faintly.

"Yeah. I looked ahead a little bit, you know, just to see what happens. Me and Joan get married not long after that," he said, and for the first time a faint smile came to his lips.

"You're a little young for that, don't you think?" I asked, and he shrugged.

"Maybe, but I'm old enough to keep a promise," he said.

Well, there was that. Cam wasn't the type to go back on his word; he never had been. And Joan wasn't either, from all that I knew of her. I suppose there are times when even a seventeen year old can understand when he's making a solemn oath to God which will change the shape of his life forever. So maybe the two of them really would be all right, in spite of how young they were.

I should've been glad for him, I guess. All he really had here was me and Justin and Eileen and Josiah, and maybe two or three friends. Nothing he couldn't let go of, if he had to. And up there in the future was waiting for him (apparently) the girl he'd be married to. And honestly, it wasn't that I didn't like Joan. She was a good girl; brave, loyal, and truer than steel. Joan of Arc herself hadn't been made of sterner stuff than Joan Rusk, and I guess Cameron couldn't have hoped for better. It's just that I'd miss the only brother I ever had, that's all.

My mind drifted back to that day at the deer camp in the mountains when we first met, and all the things we'd been through together since then. Gun battles, car wrecks, anointing as Avengers, faith and doubt and miracles galore. I dare say we shared more blood than most real brothers do, and I guess in my heart of hearts I always thought we'd end up living side by side, like brothers often do. Or at least close enough so we could see each other once in a while. But this was forever, and I knew right then I'd never see Cameron again as long as I lived. That was a hard thing, although I suppose it was no harder than many another young man has had to face on the day he leaves home.

But still, I'd be lying if I said I didn't feel it keenly.

"But what'll you do, that far ahead? I'm sure things have changed a lot," I said, still avoiding the real issue.

"I don't know for sure. I know how to build things, and do ranch work, and stuff like that. Those things never change that much," he said.

I didn't say anything to that, and I guess he must have known how I was feeling, because he clapped me on the shoulder.

"It'll be all right, Zach. I can wait a while before I go. It won't make any difference on her end; I'll still get there at the same time, anyway. I'll wait till my birthday, at least; that's still a few months off yet. We never knew which way we'd both go after high school, anyway, so this only moves things up a little bit," he said.

That was true enough; in fact I'd just been thinking that very thing myself. But until recently I'd somehow never imagined the future might include one of us running off to the year 2135 in a time machine built by an evil scientist. No doubt the future is never *quite* what you expect, but I can't help thinking that's got to rank right up there amongst the events no sane person would ever anticipate.

It crossed my mind that we might *both* go, but it didn't take me long to realize how unworkable that was. I wouldn't have a ready-made identity to slip into like he did, and anyway I couldn't see Jolie wanting to jump off into the unknown future like that. She had too much to hold her here, and so did I.

Thinking about all those things *did* add a certain extra layer of poignancy to our vacation, though, to say the least. It always does, when you're trying to have fun and you know the whole time that it'll be the last walk you ever take with somebody you love. You can put it out of your mind for a while, of course, but it's never far from your heart. Trust me, I know.

We ended up going to several places besides just Yellowstone. I don't remember where all, actually; it's kind of a blur of mountains and valleys and monuments. Eileen is a souvenir junkie, so I'm sure we've got a t-shirt or a fake bear claw or at least a rock from every single place we visited.

But all good things must come to an end sooner or later, so after two weeks of roaming the national parks it was time to head back home.

As usual, things didn't quite work out that way.

It was our last day in Wyoming before we headed home, and the plan was to finish things off with a two-hour dinner-and-dancing sightseeing cruise on Lake Yellowstone that evening. That's when it happened.

Justin and Eileen were dancing in the ship's ballroom while me and Cameron took turns feeding Joey and watching the scenery outside, talking about nothing in particular while we finished eating. Then all of a sudden there was a massive explosion from the back end of the boat, and immediately the room started to fill up with clouds of thick black smoke. The blast knocked everybody to the floor, of course, and it must have put a pretty big monster of a hole in the hull, too. I could already feel the ship listing towards the back, and it didn't take a genius to figure out that we'd soon be on the bottom of the lake if we didn't get out of there. *Not* a good thing.

"What happened!" Cam yelled.

"I don't know, but let's get out of here!" I yelled right back. We were still underneath most of the smoke, even though we could smell it, and we started crawling toward the exit doors that led out onto the main deck. In the meantime the floor was getting steeper all the time, and we could hear other people yelling and screaming and crying while they tried to get out or find each other.

Somebody stumbled over me and fell on the floor with a curse, and then got back up and tried to run. I wanted to tell him to get down on the floor and crawl, but I couldn't spare the breath. Things were getting pretty toxic even down low.

We finally made it to the doors and got outside onto the sightseeing deck where there was some fresher air, and none too soon, either. The boat wasn't all that big to start with, and through watery eyes I saw that half of it was already under water. Dozens of people were already in the lake, swimming away from the wreck.

Distances across water are deceptive; it's always farther than it looks, and most people can't swim nearly as far as they think they can. That's one way people end up drowning. There was shoreline all around us, but those pretty beaches might as well have been on the Moon for all the good they did us. To make things worse, we had on fancy clothes for the dinner, and that wouldn't do at all once we dropped into the water in a few minutes

You might think we were in a pretty tight spot, after hearing all that. And I guess maybe we were. But if I've learned anything over the past few years, it's to keep a cool head in dangerous situations. If you don't, then you're liable to get hurt. So I forced myself to stay calm and started stripping right there on the deck, not caring one whit if I lost my rented suit or if a bunch of strangers saw me in my underwear. Survival is a much deeper issue.

Cameron was doing the same thing, hampered by having to keep hold of Joey. He fumbled with the buttons and zippers one-handed, and in a scant few minutes we were both stripped. We jumped off the deck right before it slipped under, and found ourselves treading water amongst a bunch of other passengers.

"Don't try to swim. Float," he said, and I nodded. Thankfully the water was semi-warm, and there's really no limit to how long you can float if you need to. Hundreds of people had probably seen and heard that explosion, and that meant we'd probably have help on the way pretty soon, if we waited it out.

So we floated, and took turns holding Joey up, and waited for help to come.

"What happened, do you think?" he asked again.

"I don't know. Maybe something went wrong with the engine, or maybe there was a bomb," I said, half-jokingly. I made it sound like a joke because I really wanted him to tell me not to be stupid and to stop imagining things. My worst and darkest fear was that it had been a bomb set by one of the remaining Garzas, and I was trying my dead level best to keep from having to believe that.

He must have been thinking the very same thing, though.

"Do you think it was Gabe?" he asked.

"I hope not. I thought maybe he'd leave us alone after all this time," I said.

"Yeah, but you know how much the Garzas like bombs," he said.

I started to answer him, but that was right before something grabbed my ankle.

I barely had time to suck in a lungful of air before I got yanked under, and if you think that's not enough to terrify anybody, then give it a try sometime. I kicked and struggled to get loose but the hold on my ankle was like a steel band, and I could feel myself getting dragged deeper and deeper every second.

All kinds of crazy thoughts went through my head right then, up to and including whether or not they had Loch Ness Monsters in Wyoming or not. I didn't think so, but I couldn't imagine what else it could be that had such an iron grip and could drag me down so *fast*. No normal human being could have done it; I was certain of that.

But however that might be, I knew well enough that I only had a minute or two before I drowned, and then it wouldn't make any difference if I ended up getting eaten by a sea monster after that.

I found myself strangely calm about the whole thing, actually, even detached and methodical, almost. Maybe it's always like that, when you know there's absolutely nothing you can do to save yourself. I simply prayed God to forgive me for anything I might have done wrong, asked Him to watch over the people I loved, and prepared myself to die like a man of honor.

Thankfully it didn't turn out quite like that. Before I had time to drown, I found myself dragged up out of the water and hurled down on a metal floor. It hurt, but I hardly even noticed that; I was too busy gasping in air. I finally looked up with bleary eyes to see where I might be.

It was a boat of some kind; I could see that immediately. There were metal walls all around me lined with benches, and far across the lake I could hear the faint sounds of whatever was going on at the wreck site. But all that was secondary, because right in front of me stood a man in a wet suit.

The only time I ever saw Gabe Garza before was that night in the guesthouse in Natchitoches. The light had been bad, and I'd been too busy gasping for air after getting hit with a curtain rod to pay much attention to what he looked like. But somehow I recognized him immediately. He had dark brown hair and golden eyes the exact same color as a rattlesnake's, just like Orem did.

My first panicked thought was that it would have been a really good time to have the Guardian Stone with me. But it was locked up tight in Sarah Doucet's safe, over a thousand miles away. If Gabe wanted to kill me then I was pretty much at his mercy.

"Do sit down, Mr. Trewick. We have things to discuss," he said, in a surprisingly warm and conversational tone of voice. It was almost like we were having a nice little chat about the weather.

I got to my feet, still coughing, and mutely took a seat on one of the benches. I meant to escape if I got the chance, but in the meantime I also wanted to find out what was going on, if possible. I looked at him expectantly, not offering anything.

"Do forgive me for the nature of our meeting, but I felt it to be necessary. It's come to my attention that you've recently acquired a Guardian Stone. Is that correct?" he asked.

I tried to imagine how he could possibly have found out about that, especially so soon, and came up blank.

"I think first you should-" I began, and then he hit me. Right in the jaw, and *hard,* too. I flew off my seat and crashed to the floor again, nearly knocked out from a single punch. He was unbelievably strong. I looked up, dazed, to see him standing there just as cool and emotionless as ever. He must have been fast as a striking snake, too, because I never even saw his fist coming. I spit blood onto the metal floor.

"I'll be the one who asks the questions here, Mr. Trewick. You'll speak when spoken to. Understood?" he asked. It galled me to do it, but I gritted my teeth and nodded.

"Good. Now, to return to my earlier question. Is it true that you've recovered the Guardian Stone?" he asked.

"Yes, it's true," I said.

"That's what I thought. That might allow us to make a deal," he said.

"Huh?" I asked without thinking, and like a flash he kicked me in the side. I guess if he'd been wearing steel-toed boots he probably would have broken a rib or two. As it was, it hurt even worse than the punch and knocked the breath out of me.

"I told you I'll do the talking here, Mr. Trewick. I advise you not to test me a third time," he said. I couldn't have answered right then even if I'd wanted to. I was too busy lying on the floor trying to get my body to breathe again.

"Curiosity is sometimes a fatal character flaw, Mr. Trewick. You should learn to curb your inquiring mind. Now, attend to me. I'm willing to offer you a very simple deal. I will allow you to leave this boat tonight, alive, and in the future I will leave your family and friends alone. In return for this, you will bring me the Guardian Stone, and you will tell no one about me or this visit we've had. If you break the terms of this agreement, I will kill all of you. It's really that simple, and I *will* know if you break them. Do you understand these rules?" he asked.

"Yes," I said.

"Do you understand the consequences for breaking these rules?" he asked.

"Yes," I said.

"Good. I'm glad we understand each other, Mr. Trewick. Now, let's get you back over there before you're missed for too long. You may go," he said, gesturing toward the water.

I hesitated, and he tapped his foot on the deck impatiently.

"Go, Mr. Trewick, or I may yet change my mind," he finally said.

That decided me. I jumped into the lake and swam back towards the rescue site. It wasn't quite as far as I thought it was, but it was far enough. I don't think I could have swum very much farther. The park rangers were still picking people out of the water from the sinking. I yelled to get their attention when I was still a good distance away, and they soon came to scoop me up out of the lake.

The others were already on board the rescue boat, wrapped in blankets and sitting on the gunwale, and when Justin and Eileen saw me they got up and rushed over to throw their arms around me. I tried not to let it show how much that hurt my sore ribs.

"What happened! I thought we lost you!" Eileen cried.

"I guess it must have been the undertow," I said weakly, unable to think of anything better to say on the spur of the moment like that.

"Undertow? In a lake?" she asked skeptically, pulling away to look at me.

"I got sucked under and then popped up way over yonder; I don't know what else it could've been," I said. She looked at me for a second longer, then went back to hugging me.

"Well, whatever it was, you're safe now. That's all that matters," she said.

I really wished that were true.

Chapter Twelve

I kept my mouth shut about what happened on Lake Yellowstone, just like Gabe Garza told me to. I didn't know what to do, and the first rule when you're in a bad situation is not to do anything to make it worse.

I didn't doubt Gabe had some way or other to keep tabs on me if he wanted to. He knew too much for me not to believe that. I reasoned that he'd probably leave us alone for a while to make it easier for me to get hold of the Guardian Stone, and then when I had it, he'd find a way to get in touch. I didn't like the deal he offered me, but on the other hand I didn't know what else to do. He scared me, worse than Marc Doucet or Logan Tygart or any of the other villains I'd dealt with in the past had ever done.

On the third hand, I didn't know if he'd keep his word even if I *did* find a way to give him the Stone. He might take it and then kill all of us anyway.

The whole thing weighed me down pretty heavily, and I was preoccupied and quiet after we got home.

Two weeks later, Matthieu showed up.

I wasn't expecting him, but I knew who it was as soon as I saw his big black truck in the driveway. He parked next to Eileen's car, and when he got out I noticed he was alone. That was kind of unusual; normally Jolie wouldn't have passed up an opportunity to come visit me if she got the chance.

"So what's up, Matt?" I asked, when he sat down next to me.

"Several things, I'm afraid. We finally cracked the code on Dr. Garza's journals," he said.

"You did?" I asked, suddenly interested.

"Yeah, but it's not good," he said.

"Is it ever good, when it comes to him?" I asked.

"Well, no, I guess not. But it's bad in particular for you," he said.

"Me? Why's that?" I asked.

"You and Cameron are on his enemies list, that's why. People to be eliminated as soon as possible," he said.

"But why? I never even heard of him before, till I picked up his bottle that day," I said.

"I don't know, Zach, but he definitely thinks y'all are a major threat to him and Gabe and Orem. It was right there in his books," he said.

"But it shouldn't matter since he's gone now, right?" I asked.

"Not as far as *he's* concerned, no. But Gabe is still here, and I'm sure he knows about it, too. So does Orem, if I had to guess. But it's Gabe that really worries me. I don't know what he's been up to these past few months, but he definitely has a personal stake in this. He won't just let it go," he said.

I remembered what Cameron had seen with the tachometer, about killing Dr. Garza in Biloxi. So maybe Andrew had good reason to think *he* was a threat, although I couldn't help wondering *how* he knew. Surely if he knew specifically when and where the danger was, he would've made sure not to go there, wouldn't he?

"Do you think Dr. Garza saw something with the tachometer?" I asked uncertainly.

"I doubt it. It's much more likely that he got some kind of vague warning that you and Cam were dangerous to them. He could've used his crystal ball for *that*. It wouldn't have told him near as much, but he could've found out your name and some other bits of information that way. Not as precise as the tachometer, but much quicker and easier to use. The one thing I do know is, he had you both marked for destruction, and this is one time when Gabe will follow through with it. Self-interest was the one thing those two never disagreed about," he said.

"What about you and Jolie?" I asked.

"Gabe won't care about that right now. He'll deal with the rest of us and anybody else he hates when he's got time. None of us is any direct threat to *him*, you see. For now all he cares about is killing you and Cameron," he said.

"Yeah, no doubt," I agreed. I wondered (not for the first time) if Gabe Garza could be trusted to keep his word even if I gave him the Guardian Stone. If he hated us that much and believed we were a serious threat to him, then the answer was probably no.

But what if I didn't? I'd seen repeatedly how easy it was for Gabe and Andrew to find us when they wanted to, and how powerful and dangerous they could be. If it had been only me, I might have been willing to keep the Guardian Stone and take my chances. But when people you love are in danger, it puts things in a whole different light. So I *still* didn't know what to do.

"I don't know what to say, except to ask you to take this," Matthieu said, and stretched out his hand. In his upturned palm was the Guardian Stone that we took from the *San Andrés*.

My first thought was that Gabe might be watching us right that very minute, and that he'd show up to claim his prize before the sun went down. The very thought of it made me feel like a traitor and a hypocrite.

"I can't take that," I said automatically.

"Yes, you can. You have as much right to it as any of us do, and a lot more need. No sorcery can affect you, while you have it somewhere on your body. It'll do more good for you than it ever would collecting dust in Mama's safe. And if Gabe does show up, then we still know where it is. He's not quite as powerful as Andrew, but he's strong enough. You need protection, Zach. Seriously," he said.

"But what about Cam?" I asked.

"There's only one Stone. You'll have to share it," he said, shrugging.

"What if I lose it?" I asked, thinking how hard it would be to keep up with a loose stone like that. Pockets tear sometimes, and it's easy to forget to transfer something from your old clothes to your new ones.

"I was talking to Jolie about that earlier. My suggestion is to have it attached to a necklace, and then you can wear it all the time. In fact, it'd probably be smart never to take it off," he said.

That probably *was* a good idea, actually. Having the Stone attached to a chain might even put Gabe off for another day or two while it was at the jewelry shop. Not much time, true, but I'd take whatever delays I could get.

"Let's do it," I said.

We had to go into town to find a jewelry store, and the first respectable-looking one we came to was a place called Lucky's Jewelers. No place that has a leprechaun and a pot of gold on the front door can be *quite* respectable, of course, but it was better than the others we'd seen.

An old man was sitting behind the counter half asleep when we walked inside, and the first thing I did was to lay the Guardian Stone on the glass countertop in front of him.

"Afternoon, boys. Can I help you?" he asked.

"Yes, sir. I need to know if you can attach this to a strong necklace. Something that won't break no matter what," I said. He picked it up to look it over.

"Well, it's a bit large, but I'm sure we could figure something out. We've got tungsten chains; those are the strongest. Or we could possibly go with stainless steel if you wanted something a little less expensive. We might have to shave a little bit off the top right here-" he began, but I interrupted.

"No, I don't want it cut. Not even a little bit," I insisted.

"Hmm. . . that does make it harder. We might put it inside a cage, if you like, with the wires wrapped around the surface. That would be fairly durable, and I think it could be done in such a way as to set off the crystal nicely," he said.

"How long would it take?" I asked.

"I think we could have it done by Wednesday morning," he said.

"Sure, that'll do. And let's go with the tungsten, I think," I agreed.

"Of course. I'll have Stephanie get started on it this afternoon," he said, putting the crystal in his pocket.

"Please be very careful with it, sir. That stone is irreplaceable," Matthieu told him.

"Oh? Well, we'll make sure to take extra specially good care of it then," he said, with a good-natured smile.

And you know, I have to say they really did do a beautiful job. When I went back Wednesday afternoon to pick it up, the crystal was firmly encased in a web of silvery tungsten wire, and attached to a solid chain. I slipped it around my neck as soon as I got there, and then went home full of dread as to when Gabe would show up. I was sure it wouldn't be more than a few days at the most, and then what would I do? I still hadn't decided for sure.

That night, I had my first dream.

I remembered in the back of my mind that the Guardian Stones gave true dreams to those who held them, to guide them in the way they should go. But I hadn't thought much about that aspect of things ever since we first read about them at Matthieu's house, so that first dream caught me by surprise.

For one thing, it was incredibly vivid and realistic, almost like I was standing there myself. I knew immediately it was no ordinary dream.

I saw myself standing on a rocky ledge under a bright full moon, and in my hand was a shining sword. In front of me were two huge wolves with blazing red eyes and white fangs that glinted in the moonlight. They looked dangerous and evil, and I was soon proved correct when the larger one went for my throat.

But apparently this other me knew something about swordplay, because he fought with the wolf and at last drove the sword right through the monster's heart. He and the other one howled so loud as to hurt my ears, but even louder than the howling of the wolves I heard a deep voice that seemed to cry out from the very wind and stones, just a single word:

Truesilver!

And that's where it ended. I snapped awake, my eyes wide and hardly able to tell if I was awake and the dream had really ended. It was the most powerful thing I'd ever experienced in my entire life.

But as for what it meant, I didn't have a clue. All I knew was, it put a whole different spin on the situation with Gabe Garza. I could only believe that it had to have something to do with him, and whatever else it might mean, a scene that showed me fighting him obviously meant that I wasn't supposed to give him the Guardian Stone.

I think I knew that all along, if I'd only had the courage to remember it. Gabe was an awful enemy, yes, and he might very well kill me and everybody else for not doing what he wanted.

There was no guarantee that he wouldn't. But even if he did, it's still better to go down fighting for what's right and true, than to live forever as a hypocrite. I knew that. I guess I've always known it, in the way that all people have known it since the beginning of time. *Mors ante infamium;* death before dishonor. The battle cry of everyone from the legions of Rome to the street gangs of Houston. Everyone knows the truth of it. I was an Avenger, the heir of Barthélemy, and I had sworn an oath to God Himself to fight evil to the utmost of my power; not to make deals with it, not even under threat of death. So even if it scared me, I knew what my choice had to be. I had no business forgetting it.

"I had a really weird dream last night," I told Cameron the next afternoon.

"Oh, yeah? What about?" he asked, like it didn't interest him all that much.

"No, you don't understand. I think it was one of those dreams the Guardian Stones give, when they tell you something about the future," I said.

"Really? So what happened?" he asked, with considerably more interest.

"I was standing on a rock with two wolves in front of me, and I killed one of them with a sword, and somebody said the word truesilver," I said.

"Seems like it's pretty obvious to me. You'll have to fight some wolves with a truesilver sword. Whatever that is," he added.

"Yeah, but there's not supposed to *be* any more wolves, remember?" I said.

"Well. . . true. I hadn't thought about that. I don't know what it means, then," he said.

"I guess we could ask Matthieu," I said.

"Yeah, wouldn't hurt to ask," he agreed.

So we called him up, and at first he seemed just as confused as we were about what the dream could mean. But he did know one thing that turned out to be useful.

"Yeah, I know what truesilver is. I just don't understand what it's got to do with anything," he said.

"So what is it, then?" I asked.

"It's a metal. Like silver only much, much rarer. Harder and stronger than steel; even acid can't dissolve it. It's deadly poisonous to wolves, even more so than regular silver, but like I said I don't see what it's got to do with anything. There are no more wolves, and it's harmless as dirt to a normal human being. You could probably sprinkle some on your food and eat it, if you ground it up into powder first," he said.

"Do you know where we could get some?" I asked.

"It's also called iridium. I'm sure you could buy some online if you looked around a little bit. Might be pricey, though," he said.

"I got the impression that sword in my dream was made of truesilver," I said.

"I don't know, Zach. I've never heard of anything like that before. I can ask Papa, though; he knows more about that kind of stuff than I do. Either that, or there might be something about it in the concordance. I can look there, too," he said.

"All right. Call me back if you find out anything," I said.

"Sure thing," he agreed, and that was that.

In the meantime, me and Cam got online to see what we could scrounge up ourselves. That turned out to be a real chore. It seems that iridium is alloyed with a lot of things to make them stronger; everything from spark plugs to fountain pens. I wondered for a second if werewolves ever used fountain pens, and almost laughed. It was like one of those silly questions you get asked on psych tests sometimes. *Do werewolves use fountain pens? Do bananas chew gum?* Well, I don't know if they used them or not, but common items like that didn't contain enough metal to be worth messing with, and besides that it wasn't pure.

In fact, the only two things we could find online that were made out of pure iridium were specialized scientific crucibles, or nuggets found in placer deposits near platinum mines. The crucibles are astronomically expensive, and the nuggets are rare as hen's teeth. I looked up from the computer, discouraged.

"We'll never get either one of those things," I said, shaking my head.

"Sure we will. I know the crucible is out, but where's the closest place where we can dig up some nuggets?" Cam asked.

"Looks like California," I said. He was definitely right about the crucible being impossible to get hold of, but making a trip to California to go prospecting wasn't much better. If we'd only known, we could've made a pit stop at a mine while we were at Cape Mendocino.

"I bet we can find something else. Let's keep looking," he said. We finally did locate a place where we could buy nuggets instead of having to dig them up, but that still didn't seem like much of a weapon to me.

At six o'clock, Matthieu called back.

"Do y'all want to hear something really creepy?" he asked.

"Yeah, hit me with it," I said.

"I talked to Papa about everything, and he said my grandpa actually used to *own* a truesilver sword. Can you believe it? He had it special forged, way back when. I never knew that before," he said.

That really *was* kind of creepy, when you got to thinking about it. Especially when you thought about the fact that that sword was probably the only one like it in the entire world.

"Do you know where it is?" I asked.

"No, but I'm working on that. Can y'all come over here tomorrow and help me look? There are only a few places it could be, but it'll take some time," he said.

"Sure," I agreed immediately.

So that's what we did. We got to Natchitoches about six, and spent the rest of the evening rooting through Sarah Doucet's dusty attic and trying not to sneeze. All to no avail, because we didn't find anything except cobwebs and mouse droppings.

"Well, that didn't accomplish much," Cameron said, when we finally gave up the ghost and climbed down out of the attic, filthy and covered in dust.

"Sure it did. Now we know one more place where it's not located," Matthieu said cheerfully.

We stayed there that night so as to get an early start the next morning, and in the meantime, Matthieu told us some other things he'd learned.

"It's a replica of a Knight of Saint John sword from the Middle Ages, and there's supposed to be a matching dagger that goes with it to make a set. Grandpa had it made because he liked mythology and historical weaponry, I'm told. Real silver won't hold an edge very well so it's not much good for weapons except for ceremonial things, and he wanted a sword he could actually use in battle if it ever came to that. That's why he had it made of truesilver instead. He named it Mercy, after the sword of Tristan the Brave of Tintagel, which has belonged to every King of England since Edward the Confessor over a thousand years ago. The idea being to always remind him not to kill without need. Interesting stuff," he said.

"Does the dagger have a name?" I asked, more out of curiosity than anything else.

"Not that I know of. You can give it one if you like," he said.

"Me?" I asked.

"Yeah. It'll be yours, after all," Matthieu said.

"You're giving it to me?" I asked, shocked.

"Well, yeah. It's no good to anybody else nowadays, and obviously nobody cares that much about it anymore since we can't even find the danged thing. You're the one who had the dream about a truesilver sword, so I'm not inclined to argue with something God thinks you should have," he said. When he put it that way it was hard to disagree with him.

We found the sword the next afternoon, tossed carelessly in a box behind the water heater down in the basement. An awfully unromantic spot for such a sought-after item, I couldn't help thinking. But it was still glittering and bright even after who-knew-how-many years, with nary a scratch or a scuff. Truesilver never rusts or tarnishes, and it's almost impossible to damage it.

"Dang, it's *heavy,*" I said when I tried to pick it up. That sword felt like it was made out of lead. Literally. A man would have to have some serious muscles to swing that thing around. I'm no weakling, but I had to use both hands.

"Yeah, iridium is really dense and heavy like that. Can't be helped, though," Matthieu said. We found the dagger in the same box, and even though it was heavy, too, I could at least use it one-handed. There was no scabbard with either of them.

We took them upstairs and cleaned them off, and I have to say they were beautiful pieces of workmanship. Each one had a Maltese Cross on the hilt done in red gold, and they were just as bright and new as if they'd been forged yesterday. God only knows how much they must have cost to make; the truesilver alone was probably worth a fortune. I felt bad about taking them.

"Are you sure you want to give me these?" I asked doubtfully, looking at Matthieu again. But he only laughed.

"Yes, Zach, I'm sure. Now shut up and forget about it," he said.

"Thanks," I said.

"You're welcome. And here's something else that might help you, too," he said, handing me a book. *The Art of War*, by Sun Tzu.

"What's this?" I asked.

"It's a book of strategy and tactics. Study it and you'll learn a lot," he said. I think I've mentioned before that Matthieu is one of the best strategists I've ever met in my life, so his recommendation carried a lot of weight.

We stopped at a specialty shop in Shreveport to buy scabbards, and then got back home early enough to find an online course in Western Martial Arts that was supposed to teach sword fighting basics. I had serious doubts that we could learn anything remotely useful that way, but it was better than nothing.

The first thing the video told us was to put the real sword aside and find a wooden stick or a piece of bamboo to practice with. So me and Cam both cut ourselves a cane pole from the thicket down near the lakeshore, and then cleared out a spot behind the barn so we could practice.

Then we went at it, and I'm sure made quite a spectacle of ourselves. We didn't pull any punches, though, and by the time the day was done I was bruised and sore and even bloody in a few places. Not to mention sweaty and exhausted. I felt like I'd been breaking wild horses all day long and hit the ground a few times too often, and I'm sure Cameron was no better.

There's just something about a real sword which is truly awesome, though, and we couldn't resist getting in some practice with Mercy, too. It was a fine thing to see the iridescent glitter as that bright truesilver blade flashed in the sun, sharp and sure. I'm certain it was a fluke, but at one point I actually swung it single-handed and sliced right through a thick piece of bamboo with one stroke. I was pretty proud of myself for that particular accomplishment.

We only used Mercy against sticks and bamboo, though; never each other. I didn't want to slip up and lop Cam's head off by mistake. Hitting each other with bamboo poles hurt plenty enough already without anything like *that* to worry about.

"That's some rough stuff, buddy boy," Cam said, rubbing his arm after a particularly hard smack.

"Yeah, I know. Can you imagine what it must have been like back when they really had to fight that way?" I agreed.

"I don't think I *want* to imagine it," he said ruefully.

I guess we must have looked kind of silly out there, when you thought about it. We were a little bit old to be sword fighting with bamboo sticks like ten-year-olds, and then whining about how rough it was. I might even have laughed at myself if I hadn't been so sore all over. I never claimed to be a Knight of the Round Table or any such thing; this was just groping in the dark trying to do what I thought that crazy dream was telling me to do. Nothing would have pleased me better than to hang that shining truesilver sword above the fireplace and never use it again.

I put my hands on my knees and stretched my muscles, letting out a long breath. The sun was going down, and it was time to call it a night. I was pretty sure I learned at least a little bit from sparring all day, at least enough not to drop the sword. Any real skill would take months if not years of practice and training, and that was time we probably didn't have. If nothing else, I think I picked up a healthy new respect for my ancestors.

"So have you thought of a name for the dagger, yet?" Cameron asked, interrupting my train of thought;.

"Yeah, actually I have. I think I'll name it Sting; you know, after Bilbo's dagger in *The Lord of the Rings,*" I said.

"Sting?" Cam asked skeptically.

"Yeah. That's one of my favorite books of all time, and besides, it's a cool name," I said.

"Whatever you say, bro," Cam said, shaking his head.

Chapter Thirteen

Justin and Eileen went out that night to see a movie and have dinner, leaving me and Cameron at home to baby-sit Josiah. Not that we minded, you know; they deserved a date night once in a while. Jo-jo is a pretty easygoing kid most of the time, as long as you keep an eye on him. He can crawl around faster than a speeding bullet and anything he finds which is small enough *will* end up in his mouth, no matter how nasty, sharp, or poisonous it may be. But he always went to sleep by eight o'clock, so it wasn't such a big thing as it might sound like. I was looking forward to a quiet night of lounging on the couch to rest my aching body and maybe going to bed early myself. It was sultry and overcast by then, with storm clouds and lightning off to the west, and I hoped it might actually break down and rain for a few hours. That always puts me to sleep.

But in the meantime, I took Matthieu's advice and started reading *The Art of War*, too tired to really study it but mostly just browsing the pages to see what it was about. There was a lot of good stuff in there and I got interested in spite of myself.

But our quiet evening wasn't meant to be.

I guess Gabe must have been watching me after all, and he must have realized at some point that our deal was off. I don't doubt he chose that particular night to attack us precisely because Justin and Eileen were gone. It's always good strategy to isolate your enemies and pick them off one by one when they're alone. Or at least according to Master Sun Tzu it is, and I don't doubt the truth of it.

Cameron saw them first, loping across the front yard in the weak glow from the porch light about nine o'clock.

"Look!" he said, pointing out the window. I had to turn my head to see, but sure enough, there they were under the hickory trees; two of the biggest wolves I've ever seen in my life.

Like I said before, I'd been under the distinct impression that there were no such things as werewolves anymore, after we crushed the curse on Mont Mouchet. But seeing is believing, and I couldn't doubt what I saw right in front of my own eyes. But then, Gabe Garza was a pretty powerful sorcerer, and maybe he could still change his form like that by using his magic, even if the werewolf curse itself was broken. That's my best guess, anyway.

They were bigger than any other werewolves I've ever seen, and that also made me think maybe this was some new thing Gabe was doing with his own magic. They were *much* bigger than ordinary wolves, and thicker and heavier. One of them was dark brown and the other pale gray, but the really spooky thing about them was their eyes. Ordinary wolves have brown or yellow eyes, or some shade in between those two, and so do werewolves. Very occasionally pale green. But never red, in spite of what they show on television now and then. These wolves had eyes red as hot coals, just like in my dream.

They sat down in the middle of the yard, unnaturally quiet while they stared at the front door.

"Come out, Mr. Trewick. We need to talk," the big gray one said, and I flinched when I heard my name. It was bizarre to see human speech coming from a wolf like that. I don't think he could talk as well as he could when he was in human form, because his voice was rough and gurgly, just like you'd expect a wolf to sound. I started to unlock the door.

"What are you doing?" Cameron hissed, grabbing my arm to stop me.

"Going out to talk to him," I said coolly. I knew what he was thinking; that I'd be defenseless out there, alone against two of them. He had a point, but I didn't mean to do anything stupid.

"You can't do that!" he said.

"I'll just stand on the porch. That way if he tries anything I can get back inside real quick," I promised him. I wasn't totally sure that would work, of course; I knew how fast they could be. But I wanted to hear what he had to say, and I had Mercy in a pinch. I only hoped I might learn enough to make it worth the risk. Cameron had Sting, so at least we were both armed, just in case.

Cam let me go, and I cautiously stepped out onto the porch, keeping one hand on the pommel of my sword. I didn't want to go outside with it already drawn because I didn't want Gabe to know I had it, but I *did* want to be able to pull it out at a second's notice if I had to. I stopped three paces from the door.

"Come closer," he growled softly, when I didn't move.

"I think we're close enough, thanks. Speak your piece," I told him.

Maybe I should have known better than to parley with him in the first place; I guess the whole thing was just a ruse to get me outside. Because all he did was growl under his breath, and then both of them went for me at once.

They were terrifyingly fast. I barely had time to jerk my sword out and hold it up in front of my face before the first one was on me.

I think if I hadn't had that truesilver blade, things would probably have gone badly in a hurry. I would have been wolf meat before I could have blinked. But I slashed the gray one across the face, giving him a deep cut, and he fell to the porch floor howling and writhing in agony. He completely forgot about me after that, and the sight of him must have given the other one something to think about. He skidded to a halt not ten feet away, growling at me with his hackles raised, and I stood there with my back up against the wall, heart pounding and gripping my sword so tight I thought I might never be able to turn it loose.

"Truesilver," he spat, and I didn't say a word.

I've never seen a werewolf get poisoned with silver before, but I know dadgummed well that ordinary silver won't do a thing to ex-wolves; Jake Golden showed me that six months ago when he intentionally scratched himself with a piece of it just to prove he could. But truesilver is another thing entirely, it seems. I don't suppose the Doucets would have had any way of knowing that truesilver is still poisonous even to ex-wolves, seeing as how there have never been any of them till recently. I never would have guessed it myself if it hadn't been for that dream, and I thanked God and Madryn of Gwent profusely.

The one I cut had settled down to whimper and moan, and he seemed deathly ill. The other one ignored him.

He hadn't given up yet, though. Slowly, he started to circle around, trying to make it so I couldn't keep both of them in view. I knew what the game was, and I slid along the wall myself to grab the screen door and slip back inside. He saw what I was doing, and I guess he must have decided the time had come.

He went for my throat, and he was so close this time that I didn't have a chance to do anything. I crashed backward through the screen door when he slammed into me, hitting the floor in the living room and sliding probably ten feet or more across the slick hardwood. Mercy was knocked out of my hand to clatter all the way up under the couch before anybody could grab it. I heard somebody scream and I thought for a second the wolf was about to tear my throat out. He was so close I could feel his hot breath on my face.

Cameron saved me just in time, though. He still had Sting, and quicker than thought he plunged it right up to the hilt between the monster's ribs. The wolf collapsed on my chest, maybe injured, maybe dead, I didn't know. Sting was still buried in his side, wrenched out of Cam's grip.

That was bad, because the big gray one seemed to have recovered himself by then. He suddenly appeared in the archway of the door, growling, and now neither of us had a weapon left to defend ourselves. I couldn't even *move,* pinned down under the dead wolf and barely able to breathe from the weight. No matter how hard I struggled, I couldn't get out from under him.

But there was worse to come.

I guess Josiah must have heard all the commotion and come crawling to see what the matter was, because all of a sudden I saw him sitting there in the kitchen doorway, big-eyed and frozen in place, clutching one of his toys. The big gray wolf saw him too.

Cameron was defenseless, and on a purely tactical level I guess it would have been smarter for Gabe to take out his strongest opponent while he had the chance. But somehow I knew it was Josiah he'd go for. Matthieu had warned us several times how much all the Garzas loved pain and torture, and the temptation to make us watch Jo-jo getting torn to pieces right in front of our eyes was probably irresistible. Cam was groping frantically under the couch to retrieve Mercy, but I knew he'd never manage it before it was too late.

I saw all that in a split second, the way you do sometimes when time seems to move in slow motion. I saw the gray wolf leap off the floor, straight for Joey's throat. I grabbed Sting's bloody handle that was still stuck inside the wolf and yanked it out, and even though it was hardly the Dixie League World Series, I took the best aim I could and threw the blade fast and hard. If all those years of baseball practice ever taught me anything, I prayed they'd pay off now.

The dagger flew across the room, flashing in the light from the kitchen, and for a horrible second I thought I'd missed him. I almost *did* miss, as a matter of fact. The very tip of the blade sank in about half an inch right in front of his back leg, down low where the hair was thin on his belly.

It fell out immediately, of course, and if it had been a normal dagger then it wouldn't have been enough of a wound to sneeze at. But it was enough. He fell to the floor howling in agony, just like he did before, all thought of attacking anybody seemingly forgotten.

Cameron had snatched Mercy back out from under the couch by then, and ignored the writhing wolf on the floor to grab Joey from the kitchen doorway. Then he came over to help roll the dead one off my chest. Both of us together finally managed it, and I struggled to my feet covered in wolf's blood.

"Come on, let's get out of here!" I said, heading for the front door. If the past was any guide, it wouldn't take long before Gabe recovered from such a piddly little wound as I gave him with the dagger. I don't know exactly what truesilver does to an ex-wolf, but it obviously took more than a cut or a scratch to cause any lasting damage.

I guess we could have used the sword to finish him off. Maybe it would have been the smart thing to do, even. But I remembered what Matthieu had said, about how you should never kill without need. To do it while defending yourself and the people you love is one thing; to do it in cold blood while your enemy lies helpless at your feet is a different thing altogether.

"What about *him?*" Cam asked, nodding his head at the gray wolf in front of the fireplace.

"Never mind him. Let's *go,*" I said.

I guess Gabe was still too sick to get up, but he growled at me just before we went out the door. I glanced back to see him staring at me with his coal-red eyes, and for a second we locked gazes.

"It's not over," he snarled. That was exactly what I feared, but I didn't say a word to answer him.

And it *wasn't* over; not by a long shot. Because no sooner did we get outside than the reinforcements arrived. It was dark as a tub of sorghum molasses outside, with the storm clouds from earlier almost right on top of us by then. We almost ran right into the midst of the zombies before we even realized they were there.

We both skidded to a stop, appalled. Gabe must have been busy all this time, building up an army of soldiers to follow him. There were dozens, maybe even hundreds of them, shuffling out of the dark from all directions, and behind us was a murderous sorcerer with a bad attitude and a score to settle. Add to that a scared and screaming baby and maybe you'll realize how I felt right that second.

There was no way we could reach the truck.

There was no way we could fight that many enemies out in the open.

We didn't dare go back inside the house.

"Head for the barn!" I cried, and that's what we did. If we climbed up to the hayloft, there was a chance we could hold them off for a while.

Zombies are not very fast, but I have to say they're awfully determined. It wasn't long before we found ourselves in a pitched battle to keep them out of the loft. The only weapon I had was Mercy, and Cam had had the good sense to grab his aluminum baseball bat from beside the front door when we left the house. Next to a sword, that was probably the best weapon anybody could've asked for. All you can do with monsters like that is to knock their heads off or beat them to pieces.

We hacked and pounded and slashed and hammered them till we were exhausted, and still there were more. Some of them were throwing things at us; sticks and rocks or whatever else they could get their grubby hands on, while others kept trying to climb the ladder or even the outside walls. A few of them were busily stacking up bales of hay so they could climb into the windows at both ends of the loft, and that was a bad, *bad* thing.

To make things even worse, the storm finally broke, with strong wind and drenching rain, and I guess Gabe must have used it to his benefit, because all of a sudden a bolt of lightning struck the roof of the barn, showering us with fire and bits of charred wood, and then heavy rain pouring in through the hole it left behind. I knew it was Gabe's doing, because soon enough it happened again, and then again. If it hadn't been for the rain the whole barn would've been in flames by then, and as it was the roof was already starting to look like Swiss cheese. A few more strikes like that and it would either collapse on top of our heads or else Gabe would finally have a clear shot to incinerate us with another bolt.

Joey was wailing again from where we'd stuffed him into a gap in the hay bales, and I couldn't blame him. I felt like doing a little wailing myself, to be honest.

We were still fighting off all those hordes of zombies, but sheer numbers will overwhelm any defense after a while, no matter how good you are. There's no way for two people to defend three openings, either. We were about to find ourselves surrounded, and then we were done for. It was beginning to look like a choice between getting torn to pieces or burned alive, and believe me, that's not much of a choice.

If we didn't try something else we were goners, but I couldn't think what to do to save my life. Literally.

One of the principles in *The Art of War* is to know your enemy, to be so thoroughly familiar with the way he thinks and feels that you can guess what he will do in any given situation. Easier said than done, of course, but since we were about to be dead meat in very short order if I didn't think of something, it was worth trying just about anything.

So what did I know about Gabe Garza? Well, other than the fact that he hated me, I knew he was smart, ruthless, and patient, and I knew he took pleasure in cruelty.

That might be important to know; a man who enjoyed suffering and fear would want to be somewhere within sight of this battle, so he could savor it. Probably right up in the very thick of things, as a matter of fact, and that gave me an idea.

If I could find Gabe then we might be able to attack him directly and maybe even have a slim-but-real chance of living to see another sunrise. But then on the other hand, I knew he wouldn't be stupid enough to be standing down there without some kind of camouflage.

In fact, my best guess was that he'd probably used his magic to make himself look just like one of his zombies. Heaven knows there was no shortage of *them* to blend in with. But if that was the case, then how could I ever tell him apart from his soldiers? It seemed impossible.

I scrutinized the zombies which were at the bottom of the hayloft ladder, at least as well as I could in the flashes from the lightning. They all looked pretty similar at first glance. But after paying careful attention, I noticed that one of them seemed to be at the center of the action, so to speak. I don't know how Gabe controlled his minions, but it's a weakness of any commander that he can only see things from his own viewpoint, and move things in relation to himself. Now that I saw it, I also noticed that that one didn't seem to be pressing forward quite as enthusiastically as the rest, and occasionally he'd glance up at the battle, as the others never did.

I didn't stop to think about it too long or I might not have had the courage to do it. I gripped Mercy a little tighter and jumped down through the ladder hole, leaving Cameron to fight off the zombies alone.

I hit the floor and stumbled, but didn't quite fall. I knew I only had seconds to come to grips with Gabe before he redirected some of his zombies my way, and then I'd never get anywhere near him before they tore me to shreds. Speed and surprise were my only allies.

He must have guessed I'd found him out, because he immediately dropped the disguise, held up his left hand, and then threw one of those balls of white fire at me, just like Andrew did at the motel. But I still had the Guardian Stone around my neck, and I never doubted that it would protect me. And so it did; I don't know how to describe what happened, but the fireball *splashed* all around me like water, burning the clothes of the nearest zombies and catching some stray wisps of hay on fire. But none of it touched me at all.

Gabe Garza looked at me with hate in his eyes, but instead of trying to run he turned and threw another bolt of fire at Cameron and Joey instead. No more cat and mouse games, it seemed; no more playing with us so he could enjoy our despair. He was ready to end it.

That was the last thing he ever did, though, because just as the fiery bolt left his hand I plunged my truesilver blade right into his black heart. His eyes blazed red for a split second, and then winked out as he fell at my feet.

Several other things happened right then, too. The zombies suddenly went slack and unmoving, just standing there like empty shells. And the bolt of fire that almost surely would have charred Cam and Joey to cinders if I'd been even a second slower crackled and flamed out before it quite reached the top of the ladder.

It doesn't sound very brave, I know, but the first thing I did after that was to turn aside and throw up. It may sound like it's easy to kill a man, but I promise you it's not. Even when I knew it was just and right, it was still no easier.

Cameron climbed down the ladder with Joey in his arms, keeping as far as possible from the silently standing zombies. Then we all three got out of there faster than arrow from a hickory bow.

We drove downtown to the movie theater after that, and I'm sure all three of us must have made a hideous sight, covered in blood and smoke and sweat, our clothes and hair matted with rainwater. Joey was asleep between me and Cam without his car seat or even a belt on, and I could only pray we didn't get pulled over for anything. I couldn't imagine how we'd ever manage to explain ourselves.

I called Justin and Eileen to let them know what happened, and they rented a motel room instead of going back home that night. I don't think any of us could have faced that, after the ordeal we'd just been through.

* * * * * * *

Nothing had changed when we ventured back home in the morning. The zombies were still standing there quietly, and Gabe and the dead wolf were exactly where we left them. I could only assume the dead wolf was Orem; I couldn't think of anybody else Gabe could have recruited for something like that. But there was no way to tell for sure.

We burned the zombies in a big bonfire in the horse pasture, and then scattered the ashes into Coca Cola Lake. I don't know who those people were, or where they came from, or when or how they were so unlucky as to meet up with the Garzas. I don't suppose any of us will ever know, and to be honest I'm not sure I want to. But me and Cam and Justin and Eileen all held hands in a circle and prayed for them down there on the lakeshore, whoever they might have been, and committed their souls to God who is Love.

Then we started in on the long clean-up process, fixing the smashed-in screen and the dried blood on the floor and the well-nigh ruined barn roof and all the rest of the damage that had been done. It took a while, but by the time school started back for the year there wasn't much to show that not long ago the place had been the site of a pitched battle with hordes of zombies and smoke and fire and destruction.

I prayed it would turn out to be the *last* time it was the site of a battle like that.

But for now at least, it was finally over.

Chapter Fourteen

Or maybe not quite.

Things were quiet for about two months, and then me and Cam decided to go on a hiking trip in the mountains one day. Nothing very unusual about that. There's a particular knot of tall and rugged peaks which both of us had always liked especially well, just north of a little spot in the road named Langley. It's a really wild and scenic area, and there are a lot of rivers that begin up there and come flowing down as whitewater rapids and stair-step falls. It's a good place to go rafting, and it's not far from there that I killed my one and only black bear, on a hunting trip with Cameron and Levi two years ago.

I remember the leaves were changing, red and gold and russet brown. It smelled like fall, and it felt like a perfect Indian summer day; warm and dry and breezy. Good hiking weather. So we hiked and climbed and scrambled our way up to the very summit of Mount Blaylock, and sat on a boulder up there for a little while to enjoy the view while we drank a Coke and let the wind dry the sweat from our faces. The Ozarks are gentle mountains, mostly green and leafy all the way to the top unless there's not enough dirt up there for anything to grow. Blaylock is only a two thousand foot climb all the way from base level up to the summit. But it's dadgummed steep nevertheless, so you definitely get your workout for the day.

I wasn't thinking about danger. It was mostly a chance to do something fun with Cam while I still could; his birthday was coming up fast, and after that he'd be gone.

In fact, everything was peachy till about five o'clock that evening.

We were already on our way back down to the truck by then, pleasantly tired and starting to think about supper and a bath. We stopped to rest beside the trail for a few minutes, and I went off into the woods to answer a call of nature.

We were still about a thousand feet above base level, I guess, and I was looking out across the ridges and valleys while I watered the grass. I wasn't thinking about much; you rarely do at times like that. Off to the west was the Cossatot Range, a name I've always particularly liked because it means "skull-crusher". The river of the same name that comes down out of those mountains would certainly make you think the description is appropriate, if you'd ever seen it at certain times of year.

As it turned out, my wandering thoughts about the Skullcrusher Mountains might have been a little bit *too* appropriate.

My attention was suddenly snapped back to reality by the crunch of a twig right behind me. I glanced over my shoulder without thinking, just in time to keep from getting my own skull crushed by a rock held in the hands of a man who'd been within seconds of braining me with it. I stumbled out of the way just in time, and then almost before I knew it I was locked in a vicious scuffle with somebody whose main purpose in life seemed to be to get his hands around my neck and choke me to death.

He was wearing a ski mask in spite of the warm day, and for some reason that was more unnerving than anything else. If I'd had time to think about it (which I didn't), I would've realized the only reason he could possibly have had for wearing something like that was because he didn't want to be recognized, and that therefore he must be somebody I knew. But all I had time to think of right then was fighting for my life.

The dude was a pretty tough customer; I'll give him that much, but I've been in my own share of fights these past few years, too. He kept trying to grab the Guardian Stone for some reason, and when his bare hand touched the crystal I heard a sizzling sound like when you toss hamburger meat onto a hot grill. He grunted in pain, but that didn't stop him from trying again.

We fought and struggled and kicked leaves and sticks and dirt everywhere, and somehow got a lot closer to the edge during all this than we should have. Then before I knew it we were both rolling downhill quite a bit faster than I would have liked.

It's really hard to stop yourself from tumbling down a steep slope, you know, even when you're hitting rocks and things now and then to slow you down. It wasn't quite a cliff, but it was darned close. We rolled and bounced and partly fell at least a hundred feet or maybe even more, and finally hurtled off the edge of a little bluff in a shower of gravel and stones and splashed into a shallow creek. Then the fight went on just like before.

I finally saw an opening, and hit the dude in the jaw with all the strength I could still muster. I'd been practicing with Mercy the past two months, and if that heavy sword never did anything else for me, it sure did build me up some muscle. The dude teetered for a second and then collapsed at the edge of the water while I stood there breathing hard, bruised and bloody from the trip down the mountain and hardly daring to believe it was over.

I didn't waste time catching my breath, though. I immediately went to my adversary and pulled his mask off to see who it might be.

Orem Garza.

I stared at him for a second, stunned. There was no mistaking him, though; he was still the same ugly-faced little worm I'd seen at the jail in Natchitoches. I guess I shouldn't have assumed that other wolf with Gabe must have been him, because obviously it hadn't been.

I scowled at him, wondering what to make of his sudden reappearance. It was obvious he wanted the Guardian Stone, even if I didn't yet know the reason why. His hands were scorched and burned in several places from trying to grab it, so the book we read at Matthieu's house must have been right about how it wouldn't tolerate the touch of a person with evil intent.

I couldn't help wondering what possible good a Guardian Stone would ever be to someone like that, but there had to be *some* kind of reason why he and Gabe both wanted it so badly. I finally had to shake my head and give up trying to guess. Eileen always likes to say you can't make soup from gravel, by which she means you can't form any meaningful theories when you don't have enough information.

I didn't know what to do with Orem. There was no way to tie him up, and no way to carry him out of there, either. I decided reluctantly there was nothing I could do except leave him where he was and get out myself. I hated letting him get away without knocking some answers out of him, but at least I'd know to be on guard from now on.

I resisted the urge to spit on him before I left, and started the long and difficult process of climbing back up to where Cameron was.

I met him about halfway up, picking his way down to find me. When he saw the shape I was in he stopped and stared.

"What happened?!" he cried.

So I told him all about it while we walked. The fight up top must not have taken as long as it seemed, because he said by the time he got there to see what was happening I'd already rolled off the edge.

I must have twisted my ankle a little bit at some point in the fight or the fall, and that slowed us down. I felt like I'd been in a three-ring boxing match with a gorilla, actually, but I tried not to grumble about it too much. It was way past dark by the time we made it back down to the truck, but that couldn't be helped.

"I wonder who that other wolf was, if it wasn't Orem," Cameron said.

"I don't care who it was, honestly. Maybe it was Layla, or maybe Gabe had some other low-life buddy he scrounged up. Who knows?" I said.

"But why do you think Orem wanted the Stone? I don't see what good it would do him," he said.

"Beats me, but I know he kept grabbing for it the whole time we fought. Burned his hot little hand like a wiener on a grill, too," I said.

We finished making our way back down to the truck, and once we got to an area that had phone service, I called Matthieu.

"Orem's back," I said, getting right to the point.

"I thought he was dead," Matthieu said.

"Yeah, well, apparently not. He tried to choke me to death and steal the Guardian Stone not even three hours ago," I said.

"Where is he now?" Matthieu asked.

"I don't know. I left him on the side of Mount Blaylock, but I'm sure he's long gone by this time," I said.

"But you're sure he was trying to steal the Guardian Stone?" Matthieu asked.

"Yeah. It burned his hands several times when he tried to grab it. But it's not just him, though. Gabe wanted it too. What's the deal with that?" I said.

"Hmm. . . I don't know about Gabe, but I'll tell you what I think about Orem. He's always been jealous because he's the only one in his family who can't do magic. If I had to guess, I bet he's trying to collect anything he thinks is magical, so he can set himself up and pretend to be a little tinpot magician," Matthieu said.

When he put it that way, it made Orem sound grotesquely pathetic more than anything else.

"Dang, boy, you're almost making me feel sorry for the dude," I said.

"I wouldn't go *that* far, if I were you. You shouldn't think he's any less evil than the others just because he's too weak and stupid to be effective at it. One reason he always made such a good flunky was because he liked the feeling of being a part of worse wickedness than he'd ever be able to manage on his own. No, I don't feel sorry for Orem at all," he said.

I'd never thought of it that way before, but I guess Matthieu was right. There *are* people like that; toadies and wannabes who are too feeble and dimwitted to accomplish anything themselves, but they love to participate vicariously through what other people do. All bullies have their hangers-on. All tormenters have their suck-ups and tale-bearers. The heart is just as black either way.

"So what do you think we should do about him?" I asked.

"Never mind. Keep your eyes open in the meantime and we'll track him down sooner or later, now that we know he's still out there. Like I said, he's definitely not the sharpest knife in the drawer," he said.

And with that I had to be content.

* * * * * * *

We hadn't told anybody about Cameron leaving yet, not even Matthieu and Jolie or the kids at school. He didn't want to have to explain himself ten or twenty times, and I guess nobody could blame him for that. Jake and Levi were the only two friends he meant to tell anything at all, and even then not till the night before.

But Matthieu and Jolie were a little bit different ballgame. He was still an Avenger, after all, and that carried responsibilities. He owed them an explanation for why he couldn't continue, so when they came up from Natchitoches to visit for his birthday, we decided the time was right.

Cam was born on Groundhog's Day, which is early spring in our neck of the woods. Still chilly sometimes, but the grass is starting to turn green and the first of the little wildflowers are blooming in the pastures and hedgerows. We were sitting out in the barn, enjoying the nice weather and talking about this and that, when Cameron decided to bring up the subject of leaving.

"You know, I think I should give this back," he said, taking the Ring of Sebastién off his finger and handing it to Matthieu.

"You're quitting?" Matthieu asked, sounding shocked. As well he might; people didn't normally give up being Avengers after only a few months. Not unless there was a seriously good reason.

"Well, yeah. I won't be here anymore to do it," he said, and then went on to explain where he was going and why.

"I see," Matthieu said, and then there was a long pause.

"I don't know of any reason why you should have to give up your place because of that, unless you want to. There'll surely still be evil in the world then, and still a need for Avengers to root it out. Not only that, but hopefully the other five rings will still be passed down to other people till then. Go find those people when you get there; you'll need some friends and helpers, you know," Jolie finally said.

"Yeah, she's right. They might even make you the leader. You'll definitely be the oldest member by then," Matthieu said. It was kind of a joke; the oldest Avenger is always the leader, but that's mostly a ceremonial thing. He anoints new members and assigns cases, and a few other minor functions like that, but nothing special. Jolie's father Rob was the leader at the moment. But in spite of all the years Cam would have behind him, he'd still only be eighteen in real-time, and I couldn't foresee any future group of Avengers making him the leader at that age. But I guess you never know; Rob is a stickler for protocol, and the ones in the future might be, too.

"All right, then, I'll keep it," Cameron agreed, and took back his ring.

"You definitely need to take the Guardian Stone with you, too," I said, pulling the chain from around my neck.

"Well. . . don't you think *you* might need it? Orem is still out there, you know. I don't want y'all to be unprotected, especially if he's collecting magical items," he said.

"Orem is nothing compared to the others. And besides that we already know you had the Stone, or Andrew would've burned you to a crisp that day in Biloxi," I reminded him.

"Well, that's true," he agreed, frowning.

"I think I've got a better idea," Matthieu said.

"Do tell," I said.

"Well, you remember that third Stone, don't you? The one we couldn't find?" he asked.

"Yeah, what about it?" I asked.

"I know where it is, now. It belongs to a boy named Cody McGrath, just this side of Longview. If Cam took that one, then you could both have one. Problem solved," he said.

"What, you mean it's not guarded by a tribe of hungry cannibals on top of Mount Everest, or something like that?" Cameron joked.

"Ha, ha, very funny. No, so happens it's been sitting right there under our noses for over a hundred years. Who would've thought it?" Matthieu said.

"How do you know all this?" I asked.

"It'd be a long story, but suffice it to say Cody was one of the names on that list we found on Dr. Garza's hard drive, so I went to have a word with him back in June and to offer some help if he needed it. Never heard a peep out of him till two weeks ago. Then he finally called me for help, and come to find out Layla Garza attacked him way back in October. I wish he would've told me sooner. But then it turned out he had that Guardian Stone and didn't even know what it was. It's been kind of a wild time," he said.

That was nothing unusual, I thought to myself. Matthieu lived and breathed for that kind of thing.

"So you think he'd let us have it?" I asked. It seemed doubtful that anybody would give up an item like that, but I guess you never know.

"Well, that's the catch. You'll be glad to hear that he used it to neutralize Layla. She's got no more magic than a kitten, now. *But,* that particular Stone can never be touched as long as she's alive or it'll set her free again, and nobody wants that," he said.

All these tantalizing tidbits threatened to lure me down a rabbit trail that had nothing to do with the subject at hand, but I resisted the temptation to ask what happened and how Cody got tied up with the Garzas and all that good stuff. I wonder sometimes about the stories of all the people the wolves were involved with over the years, and what must have happened to them. I know sometimes it must have turned out badly, and that's sad. But others broke through and did all right for themselves, and those are the stories I really like to hear when I can. I might not want to know very much about the Garzas' victims who never got away, but the ones who fought back and survived are kind of inspirational, you know. I would have liked to hear Cody's story.

But not right then.

"So what good is it to mention it, then?" Cam asked.

"Well, I meant to tell y'all what happened with Layla anyway, as soon as I got a chance. But here's the thing with that Stone. We can't touch it right now, true. But we're talking about way far in the future, remember? Wait and pick it up when you get there. Layla Garza will be long gone by then," he said.

"Do you think it'll still be there after all that time?" I asked doubtfully.

"I don't see why not. This one sat there on the *San Andrés* for over four hundred years before we picked it up," he said.

I considered it, and decided he might have a point.

"We'd still have to ask Cody, though," I said, and Cam nodded. I guess technically we wouldn't have *had* to ask him, since I'm sure he'd be long gone by then too. But it seemed like the right thing to do.

"Come on, then. Let's go ask him," Jolie said, getting up.

"Where does he live?" I asked.

"Avinger. Maybe forty-five minutes down the road," Matthieu said.

"Yeah, I think I know where that is," I said.

So we all four loaded up in Matthieu's truck and rode down there, talking about nothing much in particular.

Cody McGrath lives way back on a dirt road in the middle of nowhere, on a ranch named Goliad. It's a pretty place, with white wooden fences and some big pecan trees in the yard. It reminded me a little bit of Jeb Barling's ranch, actually; the first green grass of early spring just beginning to soften the fields, and a herd of black cows grazing far off by what looked like the line of a river. Matthieu had been there several times, it seemed, and he told us certain things as we drove along, pointing out this or that feature. The names were old, like places far away in time. Mount Nebo. Cadron Creek. The Land of Gilead. It made me think of all those pioneer families who went out to conquer the frontier with nothing but a flintlock rifle in one hand and a King James Bible in the other.

I like places like that, with their own strong flavor.

"Cody happens to be a very distant relative of y'alls, interestingly enough," Matthieu commented after a while.

"Really? How distant?" I asked, mildly curious.

"Twelfth cousin, I think it would be," he said.

"*Twelfth* cousin?" I asked. I didn't know they even counted that high.

"Well, yeah, but I told you it was distant. Not enough to matter, normally, but in this case it might. Because the one ancestor you happen to have in common is Daniel Trewick," he said.

"Really?" I asked again.

"Yeah, really," he said.

"I wonder if he's got blue eyes," I said, only half jokingly.

"As a matter of fact he does. But you'll see," he said.

And so we did. Cody McGrath *did* have blue eyes, just like mine and Cam's; the mark of a curse-breaker. He was younger than I expected, too; early twenties at the most. I couldn't help wondering if Daniel Trewick had any *other* seventh-generation grandsons out there that nobody knew about yet.

He was nice enough, though. Once he understood the situation he never hesitated.

"Sure, you can have the Stone once you get there. Just keep it safe, that's all I ask. I wouldn't want anything to happen to it," he said.

"I'll guard it with my life," Cam promised staunchly.

"Well, you don't have to go quite *that* far, but do be careful with it," Cody said, laughing a little.

"Thanks, Cody," Cameron said.

"No problem," Cody said.

"Where do I have to go to find it?" Cam asked.

"Do you know where Possum Kingdom is?" Cody asked.

"Yeah, I think so. It's out there close to Fort Worth, right?" Cam asked.

"Yeah, that's the one. Go out there to the Possum Kingdom dam, and follow the river downstream maybe a quarter of a mile till you come to a deep place with a boulder at the bottom of it. The Stone is inside a metal box cemented inside that boulder. You ought to recognize the spot; I'm sure the cement won't be quite the same color as the rock," Cody said.

No one asked him why it was there, even though I wondered. Presumably it had something to do with Layla Garza since it couldn't be moved, but that was all I knew. It seemed like a bizarre place to put it, but no stranger than a hundred other things I've heard in my life, I guess.

Cameron and Cody shook hands, and then we didn't stay there much longer after that. Cody had things to do, and so did we for that matter.

"That didn't take long," I commented after we left.

"I didn't think it would. Cody's a good dude," Matthieu said.

"We'll have to use the tachometer and look for a time when the river is low and there are no people around, so Cam will have a chance to dig it out," Jolie said.

And so it was. We found a day in June of 2135 when the river was low, about a week before Dr. Garza was scheduled to attack Joan, and we checked to make sure there wouldn't be any untimely releases from the dam.

We had a long debate about whether it was possible to save Philip or not, after we'd already watched him get obliterated. Knowing the future is useful sometimes, but it's also downright *weird* once in a while. It brings up all kinds of conflicts like that, about free will and whether you're able to change your mind after you've already seen yourself doing whatever-it-is. I tell you, it's enough to give you a headache just thinking about it.

We finally decided it might not be very smart to test the idea, for reasons that might seem complicated at first blush, but I suppose I'd better try to explain them.

Justin told me once that it's perfectly all right to pray about things which took place in the past, as long as you don't know what the outcome was. Such as, you could pray that your mother survived a plane crash that happened two hours ago, as long as you don't actually know whether she did or not. Once you know, that's your answer. But the same thing holds true for things that happened hundreds or even thousands of years ago, or things that will happen hundreds of years from now. God is outside of time completely, and therefore so are your prayers to Him. In that way, it's quite possible for you to be the partial cause of something that happened long before you were even born. Nothing at any point in time is outside your reach because nothing is outside His.

But for that very reason, looking through the tachometer at the future was like looking at God's will revealed. You can't change it because your own free choices are already built into what you saw in the first place. Whatever you choose, that's the result it will lead to.

I never imagined that someday I'd find myself involved in a deep discussion about the theological aspects of time travel, but then, I don't imagine anybody else ever would have imagined such a thing either.

The result of the matter was that we made two major decisions. First, that Cam would have to go along with whatever he'd already seen, and second, that we wouldn't look at the future anymore unless it was absolutely necessary. It caused too many problems.

Cam spent the next few days packing up a few things he wanted to take with him. His bullet necklace from Tennessee. A few pictures and clothes. The leather Bible that Justin and Eileen gave him. A Texas Rangers baseball pennant. Annabelle Rusk's dust bottle and the water to wake her with. A hammer to break open the rock at Possum Kingdom. It didn't seem like a lot.

"You're not taking much," I commented, watching him.

"I won't need much. Just a few of the things I can't replace," he said quietly. There was a kind of strained awkwardness between us that I hated, but I couldn't figure out how to get rid of.

"In fact, I want you to have this, Zach," he said, handing me the bullet necklace.

"Aw, Cameron, I couldn't take that," I said, knowing it was one of his most prized possessions.

"Sure you can, because I'm giving it to you. Somethin' to remember me by," he said with a smile, and oh, that stung.

"Where do you think y'all might go when you get there?" I asked, to hide my discomfiture.

"Not sure. Maybe somewhere down on the Gulf, you know. . . I like the beach. Galveston or Tampa or someplace like that. Just depends," he shrugged.

Three days later we took him out to Possum Kingdom, dressed in clothes that wouldn't look too outlandish in 2135. Then Justin put his hands on his head and blessed him and asked God to use him for something great, and to give him happiness. Then we all hugged him for the last time, and Justin and Eileen kissed him, and he picked up Josiah and got a wet smack from him, too.

There was nothing more to be said at that point, so he slung his backpack across his shoulder and walked a little way off, his tennis shoes crunching on the gravel. The tachometer was already set for the precise moment he needed to arrive. He looked back at us and waved one last time, and then he pressed the button.

He disappeared instantly with a sharp *crack* of displaced air, leaving a smoking red crater in the dirt just like Joan had left in the floor of the hotel. But there was no one around to see or hear anything except us, so it didn't much matter. I went to fetch the tachometer from the bottom of the crater where he'd dropped it, and silently reset the controls so we could watch him arrive.

Thus we turned from reality to a grainy black-and-white image, and sure enough, there he was. Some of the bushes and rocks were different, but that was about it. He waved at us, knowing we were watching him, and then carefully climbed down the riverbank to find the Guardian Stone that would protect him from Dr. Garza.

He found the place without too much trouble, and he wasn't particularly careful about pounding chunks of rock away. It took him well over an hour to hammer his way down to where the steel box was set into the stone, and when he reached it he pulled it out and held up the crystal for our benefit, so we could see that he had it. It was hung on a chain, just like mine, and he quickly slipped it around his neck. Then he waved one last time and started hiking east, towards Biloxi and whatever future awaited him. But Joey was getting antsy by then, and there was nothing left to see.

"Let's go," Justin said quietly, and so we did.

It was a quiet trip home, I have to say that. I tried to be glad for him. I think he really loved Joan, and people have done costlier things than he did for the sake of love. She came from a time when people got married even younger than we are, so that's natural for her. And as for Cameron, well, I think that's sort of what he's always wanted out of life anyway. And like he said himself, he was old enough to keep a promise.

So I told myself things were exactly as they should be, and I tried not to miss him too much. But that's harder than you think. Ever since I was fourteen years old Cameron had always been there, and when you've been that tight with somebody for that long, it leaves a big empty place in your life when they disappear. I had a big Cameron-shaped hole in my life, and it was hard to think how to fill it.

I could watch him, of course, and for a little while I did. I was there (sort of) when he married Joan on the beach in Gulf Shores. I was there when they woke up Annabelle, who looked so much like her sister that they might have been twins, almost. Cameron slipped right into Philip's empty shoes and got a job with a construction company, rebuilding houses in Tampa after a hurricane. I was there when their first baby was born a year later, blond and blue-eyed, just like Cameron. They named him Christopher, and I guess nobody but me and Cam would have known that that was supposed to be *my* name, if Mama and Daddy hadn't changed their minds at the last minute. I knew what he meant by picking that name for his first-born son, and if it's possible to feel touched and sad both at the same time, I guess that's how I felt. I watched him building houses and coaching Little League and playing with his baby boy and laughing with Joan and being happy. I was there to see all those things, just like any loving brother would have been. But it wasn't the same, and never could be.

That's as far forward as I went, though. I didn't want to run through their whole life together, because that made both of them seem less real, I guess, like watching a movie instead of a flesh-and-blood person. It was easier to imagine that the two of them had gotten married and moved away to Florida for work, and they were still in the present day and life was going on like it should. I decided I might look in on them at carefully chosen moments over the years, to make it seem like time was passing at the same speed for all of us. They didn't seem so lifeless, then.

Justin could tell I was sad, like he always can. But all he could do was clap me on the shoulder and murmur a few words about being happy for the people you love. Sometimes there's really nothing else anybody can say.

Epilogue

I graduated on the first of June, and even though Cam wasn't there, it still felt pretty good to walk across that stage and take my diploma. I was last in line, of course; that's what I get for having a last name that starts with T, but since there were only fourteen of us it didn't really matter that much.

Mom and Lola came, shockingly enough. We talked for a few minutes, and she gave me a hug for the first time in years. It wasn't quite the way I'd always pictured things, but I guess I should be thankful for small blessings.

I asked Justin a few days ago what he thought about finally naming this old place of ours. It's only ten acres, to be sure, but I don't guess anybody ever said there was a size limit. He, being the kind of man that he is, only laughed and thought it was a great idea. So we put up an arch over the gate, and inscribed the word Truesilver across it. A little whimsical, maybe, but Truesilver Ranch does have a bold and descriptive flair, now doesn't it? I think it fits, after all we've been through. Not to mention the fact that whenever company comes over, we can point to Mercy hanging there above the fireplace and tell them a tale they'll never believe.

Not that I'll be here much anymore, after the summer's done. They offered me a half scholarship at the University of Texas, not to mention a baseball stipend. That's a pretty cushy deal, you know. I won't have to pay much for school, and I'll get four years worth of playing for the Longhorns to polish up my game for the scouts. And Jolie will be there with me, of course.

I suppose Matthieu will probably call on me now and then to do some work when he comes across evil in the world. I'm still an Avenger, after all. I'm very glad indeed that the Garzas are wiped out, but I'm not so foolish as to think they're the only bad apples who ever spoiled the bunch. Or even the worst ones, for that matter. So I study tactics, and I practice my aim at the gun range, and I make it a point to learn whatever useful skills I think might get me out of a pinch someday. You never know when you might need to know those things. If I learned anything from the Garzas, it's to always be prepared.

We did catch Orem about three months ago, actually. He was holed up in an abandoned house in Las Cruces, living on canned beans and using one of Andrew's crystal balls to spy on folks and find good times to rob them. A little tinpot magician, it seems, just like Matthieu said. We set up a sting operation, using the tachometer to find a time when we knew he'd be right in the middle of a robbery, and then we tipped off the cops. In fact we told them about quite a few of his other crimes, too. They caught him red-handed, and that took care of Orem, at least for the foreseeable future.

We took the crystal ball and smashed it. If you're going to fight people who practice sorcery, then you really ought not to start practicing it yourself, you know. Orem may have been stupid enough not to know the difference between his brothers' little toys and one of the Guardian Stones, but magic and miracles are not the same thing at all. A magician wants power and thinks he can bend the world to his own will whenever and however he pleases, good or bad. Miracles are always a gift, and they're given when God chooses, never when we do.

There's still Layla, I suppose, even though she's powerless and never seemed like much of a threat to anybody except Cody. I don't dare completely dismiss her, though. I did that with Orem and nearly ended up getting my head bashed in with a rock. I won't make the same mistake twice.

I still don't know why Gabe wanted the Guardian Stone so much, but I usually keep it locked up tight nowadays, just in case Layla or anybody else gets any ideas about stealing it. I don't *think* there are any more evil sorcerers out there in the world, but it never hurts to be careful, you know.

I'm also careful to keep Sting in a sheath on my belt at all times; it looks more or less like a hunting knife that way, if you don't pay too much attention. There may not be any more evil sorcerers, but I know for a fact there are several hundred ex-wolves out there, and it's entirely possible some of *them* might hold a grudge. In fact, Matthieu and Jolie are having truesilver knives forged for themselves and the rest of the Doucets, too, just in case.

But life isn't always about fighting and battles. I've been working for Jeb Barling again this year, baling hay and feeding the cows and such. Justin tells me I'm turning into quite the cowboy, but I only laughed. I think you never really learn how much you love a place till you start thinking about leaving it behind, and then you have a tendency to pull it close to your heart while you still can. The whole pith and flavor of the Red River Valley has gradually seeped into my bones these past few years, I guess. Or maybe some of it was always there. Mama sent me a picture a while back, of me when I was no more than five years old, riding a sheep at the county fair and decked out in my cowboy duds. Mutton-busting, they call it. I don't remember it, but that was me at one time.

I suppose Austin will be a whole new world in some ways; that's what everybody tells me, at least. But Eileen always likes to say you should bloom where you're planted, so I'll try to do that. I have too much to be thankful for, to complain too much.

I still miss Cam sometimes, but it helps to know that he's happy. It's easier to be glad for him now than it was to start with.

Life is pretty tranquil for me these days, actually, and I can't say I'm sorry for that. My world is full of cows and hay and college in the fall, and after that, who knows?

I can't wait to find out.

The End
(for now)

To continue reading The Curse-Breaker Books, you have a choice. You may start by reading about Zach's distant cousins and fellow Curse-Breakers, Brian and Brandon Stone, in "Unclouded Day". The story of these two boys will eventually lead you to Cody McGrath's fight with Layla Garza and finally to Cameron and Joan's adventures in the future, when Cam becomes the leader of all the survivors of Earth. Or, you may also go more directly to Cameron's story by skipping ahead to "Nightfall" which is Book One of the Tyke McGrath Series. Free samples of both stories are provided in this book to help you choose.

Free Sample of

Unclouded Day

Book One of the Stones of Song Series

Prologue

Among the native tribes of America, it has long been told that deep underground, in a cavern green as emerald at the heart of the world, that the blessed of God might find a fountain clear and cold, and that anyone who drank of that water might live far beyond his years, young and beautiful till the end, and that his dearest wish might come true.

Now the fame and the echo of that story have gone far out into the wide world, and many heroes and great men have searched for the Fountain in vain. It is said that DeSoto himself tried to find it, and Ponce de Leon the Lion-Hearted, and perhaps many another whose name is no longer remembered. But none ever succeeded, for the way is hidden except to those who are chosen, and found worthy.

This is the tale of a boy who found himself chosen, though no one who knew him would ever have suspected he was anything but ordinary. He was no different than any of a hundred other youngsters, except that he had a mind to dream, and faith to believe, and courage to set aside himself for the sake of those he loved.

And although he would have laughed if anyone had suggested such a high calling for him, he learned in time not to wonder at the works of God, who may often choose to lift up the weak and humble things of this world to fulfill His purposes, when the strong stumble.

Chapter One

Brian found the amulet in an old cigar box in the attic. He wasn't looking for it, or anything in particular really. He just liked rooting around up there sometimes, especially on days when Mama was in a bad mood. He'd learned long ago that it was best to disappear for a while at times like that, if he didn't want a smack in the face. Out of sight, out of mind.

She'd finally passed out on the couch around two a.m. last night, and Brian had known even then that she'd probably wake up with a killer hangover the next morning. That was never something you wanted to stick around for; not if you were smart, so he'd planned to get up early and take Brandon fishing for a while. At least till she had a chance to mellow out a little bit.

But there'd been a cold gray rain falling when he opened his eyes that morning, forcing him to rethink his plans. It wouldn't do, to take Brandon out in the weather like that; the kid was always catching colds. Bran was still two weeks shy of four years old; a bit more than ten years younger than his big brother, and Brian loved him above all things in the world.

So instead he'd come up to the attic, to root around amongst Papaw's old Army trunks for a while. The whole place was full of junk his grandfather had dragged back home from all over the world, and no matter how often Brian dug through it, there was always something new to see.

Not all of it was pleasant, to be sure. Some of Daddy's old things were up there too, here and there, and it always made Brian a little sad when he stumbled across anything like that. He hadn't seen his father since Brandon was a baby, and sometimes that still stung. His name was Crush, and Bran looked very much like him with his deep red hair the color of a ripe cherry. That was memory enough, without looking for more.

But he didn't come across things like that very often, and since fishing was a no-go, then treasure-hunting in the attic seemed like a good backup plan.

So he'd crept out of bed, leaving Brandon still asleep, and tiptoed quietly upstairs. He switched on the dusty old floor lamp before picking a trunk at random, close enough to the door that he could see if Bran woke up and came out into the hall. He'd probably sleep for hours yet after staying up so late last night, but then again you never knew.

But in the meantime, Brian pulled up a chair, threw back the rusty iron latches, and lifted the lid of the trunk he'd picked. It smelled faintly musty inside, and as usual it was full of assorted junk; a baby cuckoo clock no bigger than an apple, a set of ivory throwing knives, postcards, a beeswax candle that still smelled like honeycomb, dozens of other trinkets and souvenirs like that. They were tossed in the trunk carelessly, with no particular order; just a random jumble of odds and ends.

He found the cigar box at the bottom of the trunk under a piece of cardboard, almost like someone had tried to hide it down there for some reason. Probably no one had, of course, but the idea tickled his sense of adventure. He pulled it out and blew dust off the lid, then tore off an ancient strip of duct tape that held it closed. Inside he found some crumpled rice paper yellowed with age, and wrapped up inside it was a silver necklace with a small medallion-type amulet attached. It was badly tarnished in spite of the wrapping, but there was no doubt about what it was.

Brian was delighted; this was *real* treasure!

There were seven blue gems set in a circle around a carven picture of a flowing fountain on the front of the medallion, and there was a smooth crack that ran all the way round the edge of the back side, as if it was meant to open up like a locket. There didn't seem to be any catch or knob or button that he could push to pop it open and let him see what might be inside, but while he was looking for one he did find an inscription of some sort which he couldn't make out through the tarnish. His curiosity was strong now, though, and he wasn't to be put off by such difficulties. He spit on the edge of his shirt tail and rubbed hard until he could read the writing, but even then he was none the wiser. The words simply said *Thumb Here.*

The letters were sloppy and blocky, like someone had scratched them there with the point of a pocket knife.

"Thumb here?" he repeated aloud, thinking to himself what an odd thing that was for someone to put on a piece of jewelry. It was clear enough, though, so he shrugged his shoulders and stuck his thumb where it said, wishing the silver wasn't so gummed up and nasty. It might actually be worth something if he could get the tarnish off.

The instant he touched it, a sharp pain stabbed his hand, and he cried out wildly without thinking. It felt almost like he'd touched a burning hot coal, and he dropped the thing instinctively. He quickly looked at his thumb and saw no visible injury. It didn't hurt anymore either, and his alarm changed quickly to puzzlement. He wiggled his fingers to make sure they still worked. They seemed fine. Then he listened to see if anybody was coming to check on him after that wild cry, but the house was silent. He must not have been as loud as he thought.

He stared down at the amulet suspiciously, and then cautiously prodded it with his big toe. Nothing happened, but he couldn't help noticing that the gummy black tarnish was all gone. Silver gleamed brightly even in the weak light from the lamp, and he noticed for the first time that the flowing water in the fountain-picture was speckled here and there with tiny chips of what might have been diamonds, glittering and beautiful. It looked like someone had scrubbed the whole thing spotless in the blink of an eye.

In fact, it was almost like his wish had come true.

The thought came to him out of nowhere, and he felt a rush of excitement. Brian had always believed that there had to be something more out there than just the dull and humdrum world he was used to. So when something magical was suddenly dropped in his lap, he wasn't at all disbelieving, as some people might have been. When reality is harsh, one learns very quickly to look beyond it.

Eventually he got bold enough to pick up the amulet by the chain and examine it again, this time a lot more closely. A ring of tiny words was now etched sharply into the gleaming surface around the edge, but they were much too small for him to make out what they said and he soon gave up trying.

He thought back carefully, trying to remember exactly what he'd done. His head was full of vague ideas from a hundred fairy tales and movies about how things like this were supposed to work, but he couldn't remember doing anything special except touching his thumb to the medallion.

Well, fair enough. He'd give it a try. It was worth a hurt finger to find out the truth, if that's what it took.

He looked at his shirt tail, where the spit-and-tarnish mixture from earlier was gradually turning into a smudged brown stain as it dried, and decided that would make as good an experiment as any. Therefore he took the medallion in hand, and gingerly touched his thumb to the back. He was braced for the pain this time, and was puzzled when it didn't come. Nevertheless, he forged ahead.

"I wish my shirt was clean," he said distinctly, but this time he was disappointed. Nothing happened. Brian wasn't willing to give up just yet, though. He looked down at an old pair of socks on the floor.

"Come here," he ordered them in a firm tone. Again nothing happened, and Brian was frustrated. What was he not doing right?

He tried to think again what he'd been doing when the tarnish disappeared. He'd been looking at the medallion, thinking about how it would look if it was clean. He hadn't actually said a word, come to think of it. He'd just thought it. Okay then, so maybe he had to visualize what he wanted, instead of talking out loud. He decided to try it again.

This time he didn't say anything, just envisioned the socks rising up off the floor and landing beside him on top of the trunk lid. Now there was no doubt about it. The socks floated obligingly off the floor and came to rest beside his elbow, exactly where he'd wanted them to go. There was still no pain though, and Brian broke into a huge smile.

He was eager to try some more, but then he hesitated. Mama was somewhere downstairs, and he didn't dare let her catch him doing magic, of all things. The first thing she'd do would be to take the amulet away from him, and if that happened. . .

Brian felt a cold chill at the very idea. Mama was nasty enough already, without giving her magical powers to make things even worse. There was no way he could let *that* happen. What he really needed was a place where he could be sure she wouldn't walk in and catch him, but that was impossible as long as they were both under the same roof.

He glanced outside. The rain had stopped for now, and there was nothing to keep him from leaving the house for a while if he wanted to. Fishing was forgotten for the day, but the creek was still the best hide-out he knew of, far from Mama's prying eyes. He was sorely tempted to go snatch Brandon out of bed and slip away while they still had the chance.

Then a problem came to mind, and he hesitated. Brandon had a really hard time keeping secrets, and it wouldn't do much good to go hide in the woods to do his experiments if the kid came right back home and blabbed everything, now would it?

He thought about slipping away by himself and leaving Brandon at home with Mama for a little while, even though he didn't like the idea very much. He was pretty sure Bran would sleep for hours yet after staying up so late last night, but then again he might not. If he *did* wake up early, it was a pretty good bet that Mama would end up screaming at him for spilling cereal on the floor, or making too much noise, or some stupid thing like that. Not to mention she'd probably tear Brian to pieces for not watching him, as soon as he got back home.

Not a good outcome, either way.

Nevertheless, he was almost dying with curiosity to find out more about the amulet, and he was blessed if he could think of any other solution.

He decided to risk it, just this once.

He slipped the amulet in his pocket and crept stealthily down the painted wooden stairs, stepping lightly and near the edges to avoid creaks. A thin film of dusty grime had sifted out of the wallboards since the last time he swept, and tiny particles of dirt clung unpleasantly to the bottom of his bare feet every time he took a step. He made a face and wished for the millionth time that it wasn't so hard to keep the old place clean.

He didn't stop on the second floor, not wanting to wake up either Brandon or his mother. He wasn't sure if she'd ever roused herself enough to stagger her way to bed last night or not, but he didn't want to find out the hard way by disturbing her.

The kitchen was deserted when he got to the bottom of the stairs, and he surveyed the wreckage from last night glumly. Glasses half full of unfinished milk from supper stood huddled together on the dull green Formica countertop, and dirty plates were piled high in the sink. An empty Absolut vodka bottle lay at a drunken angle against the base of the refrigerator where Mama had thrown it, and a fleet of cigarette butts floated grotesquely in a pool of spilled beer on the floor. A slightly dried-out meatball lay in solitary splendor under Brandon's chair on a thin veneer of splattered spaghetti sauce.

There was more, but Brian had seen enough. The cleanup job would be bad enough without having to think about it ahead of time. He crept a little nearer to the archway that separated the kitchen from the living room, to see if Mama was still asleep on the sofa. She wasn't, but someone had turned on the TV, and presently he noticed muffled sounds of movement coming from the bathroom. It sounded like Mama was brushing her teeth, and before long he heard something clatter on the floor and the sound of cursing. It sounded like she was in an especially nasty mood, and he felt a strong urge to disappear again.

He suffered a fresh twinge of worry about leaving Brandon alone with her, and he glanced upstairs one last time with furrowed brow, half tempted to put off his expedition for another day.

But Brian was fourteen, and the thought of waiting for anything was hard to endure, let alone something as amazing as this. Therefore he tiptoed quietly across the faded yellow linoleum to the back door, reminding himself once again that Brandon was still asleep, and that the quicker he left, the quicker he could get back.

He shut the screen door slowly behind him, careful not to let the rusty hinges squeak too loud. It didn't seem to matter how often he oiled them, that high-pitched squeal always came back in a few days. He listened to make sure Mama hadn't noticed, and then he set off purposefully across the pasture.

He quickly covered the open ground and slipped through the rusty barbed wire fence on the far side, careful not to let his jeans or his shirt get snagged. Ripped up clothes were too hard to replace.

His bare feet crunched wetly on dead vines and pine straw as he followed the little path into the woods beyond the fence, and once or twice he had to wade through a flooded spot. That was all right, though; he knew the way. By and by the trail curved away northward, following the little valley up into the mountains, and before long he came to higher and drier ground again.

At one place, an outcrop of stone jutted out over the creek, with a beautiful view of almost the whole valley to the south and a deep swimming hole underneath where you could cannonball off the rock if you were brave enough, and beyond it there was the wooded mountainside where no one ever went. That's where Brian was headed.

He and Brandon had always called that place Black Rock, though Brian couldn't remember why. It didn't really look black, except when it was wet. It was Brandon's favorite spot when the weather was nice, because there were lots of lizards and bugs to catch while they basked in the sun, and there was a sandy beach beside the creek that was perfect for castle building. Brian liked to go there and read or throw rocks even when Brandon wasn't with him, because it was a good place to be alone with his thoughts, and in the fall he sometimes hunted on the mountainside.

Not always in the fall, actually, although he didn't like to talk about that very much. Hunting deer out of season was always risky, but there'd been several times when it was either that or go hungry. Not much of a choice, when you thought about it.

But for now, the most important thing of all about Black Rock was that Mama absolutely hated the place and never went there. Brian had no idea why she felt that way, but he was glad she did.

A low growl of thunder rolled through the dense pine woods, and he looked up at the sky anxiously. The clouds were still dark and heavy with rain, and he wondered for a second if maybe his expedition hadn't been such a good idea after all.

He hesitated again, not wanting to get soaked, but eventually curiosity pulled him onward. He could always stand under a tree for a while if he had to. It wasn't quite ten minutes later when he finally emerged from the woods and stood on top of the big stone outcrop. All around the Rock was a little meadow maybe a hundred feet across, full of wildflowers when the season was right, although at the moment it held nothing but thistles and sedge grass, most of it dead from the summer heat.

The castle he and Brandon had built last week on the sand bar had melted into a shapeless blob coated with pockmarks from the rain, and there were several fresh deer tracks coming down to the water to drink. Little bits of embedded mica twinkled on the surface of the Rock, which was still dark and wet in most places.

Brian pulled the amulet out of his pocket and toyed with it. The jeweled silver glittered like broken glass, even on such a dreary day. It was a beautiful piece of work, whoever made it. Strangely enough, there was no clasp or catch on it as you would have expected to find on a necklace. The chain was made all in one continuous piece. The only way to put it on was to slip it over your head.

Brian wasn't sure he liked that idea much. He wasn't on good terms with pain in any form, and he still remembered what had happened to his thumb earlier. It had only been just that once, sure, but what if the same thing happened to his neck or chest? He wasn't keen to find out the hard way. But a necklace is meant to be worn, and with a deep breath he whisked the chain over his head before he could change his mind.

It hung lightly around his neck, the silver disk lying flat against his heart. He grasped it in his hand and held it as far away from his body as he could before he tried anything else with it, though. Might as well be as careful as possible.

His legs were coated with mud and dirt up to the knees from the flooded path, and he could feel scattered smudges of thick red clay slowly pulling hair as they dried on bare skin. His face was slick with oily sweat, curling down in streamers from his forehead. He felt grubby, and this gave him an idea for his first experiment.

"I wish I was clean," he said, imagining himself just that way. Again he felt nothing at all, but when he looked down every particle of dirt had vanished from his body. His clothes were cool and fresh, and even his teeth felt newly brushed. Brian smiled with pleasure, more confident now. His eye fell on a nearby rock.

"Come here," he commanded it, holding out his right hand. The rock trembled and then gracefully floated into his outstretched palm. Brian laughed with delight, throwing the rock into the creek and casting his eyes about for more things to work his magic on. Nothing could have knocked a chip off his satisfaction at that moment.

He played with the amulet fondly, dreaming such dreams as would have seemed unbelievable just yesterday. But now! Now all things were possible.

The summer sun had scorched the tall grass around Black Rock into a wide field of standing hay, which not even the recent rains had been able to bring back to life. The dirt was pale and rocky, full of little white stones that looked like the bleaching skulls of field mice, and Brian eyed all these things thoughtfully.

Moving rocks and cleaning off mud was all very well, but surely there was something more dramatic and interesting he could do. The dead grass and gloomy skies didn't seem to offer very many possibilities at the moment, though.

It would have been a much different place in the springtime, full of wild flowers and swallowtail butterflies and sometimes a few deer grazing at the edge of the woods. That was Brian's favorite time of year, and for a fleeting second he wished it was March instead of September.

A wild thought entered his mind, and he began to smile at the very audacity of it. He walked slowly to the center of the little meadow, and his left hand reached up to clasp the amulet curiously. Could he do it?

"Give me spring," he whispered, conjuring up the vivid image in his mind. Before the last word fell from his lips, the meadow began to change before his eyes. The dry grass broke up into wispy fragments quickly swept away by the wind. Dormant seeds burst into new life in a spreading pool of green around his feet, sending up pale tendrils already heavy with the buds of flowers. Lavender stars peppered the ground with a sprinkle of blooms, and chains of golden daffodils appeared across the far side of the meadow.

For a second he was awed by his power, and stood staring at the changes he'd made. He thought about gathering up armfuls of the daffodils and carrying them back home to brighten up the drab old house just a little. Mama liked flowers. She might even. . . well, what *would* she do, actually?

When he stopped to seriously think about it, he realized he was dreaming with his head in the sand. Mama wasn't a fool. She knew it wasn't the right time of year for daffodils, and at the very least she'd ask him where they came from. And then what would he say?

It wasn't just the daffodils, of course. Anything strange that happened around the house might cause problems. Mama was suspicious, and he knew from experience that it didn't take much to set her off. The least careless remark, the most minor incident; anything could cause an explosion.

It came to mind again that Brandon would probably be the worst problem he had when it came to keeping the secret. He was seldom out of Brian's company, and he was way too curious about things. He just didn't understand the need to keep his mouth shut sometimes.

The cool wind had dried a sweaty trail of hair against the curve of his cheek, and Brian absentmindedly brushed it away. He turned his back on Spring, the thought of his mother having temporarily soured his taste for any more playing around. He unraveled a sprig of honeysuckle which had grown around his ankle and headed back for the downward path, feeling deflated. What good was magic if you couldn't use it?

He walked quietly into the leaf-scented shade of the hickory trees, paying no attention to anything above the tips of his toes. He was lost too deep in thought. Maybe if he was super careful and only did things Mama wouldn't notice, then he might get away with it. That was an unsatisfying compromise, but it was the best thing he could think of at the moment.

He sighed, and decided it was probably about time he headed home; he needed to be back before Brandon woke up, just in case.

While he thought thus, he felt a single fat raindrop land on his arm, and again he glanced up at the sky uneasily. This time dark thunderheads were piled up like play-doh in the west, and the wind was starting to pick up again. From where he stood, he could see rain falling in dark gray sheets maybe half a mile away, and it was moving his direction.

He made a run for it, gambling on the chance that he could make it to the house before the rain did. Brian was a fast runner, and if he'd been wearing his shoes he might possibly have made it in time.

But he was barefoot, and that slowed him down just a bit. He was crawling through the fence when the rain caught him, causing him to rip a long hole in the back of his t-shirt from trying to slip through the barbed wire too quickly. He cussed under his breath and ran across the pasture to the back door, angry at the fence, and the rain, and himself most of all. He didn't have so many shirts that he could afford to tear them up like that.

He quickly got a grip on himself as he reached the house, though. There were worse things in the world than holey shirts, and the slightest display of bad temper was as sure a way to provoke Mama to anger as he knew of.

He scuffed his feet and made sure to let the screen door slam (but not too loudly, of course) when he walked into the kitchen. If he made a little noise he could let Mama know he was there without actually having to speak to her. She was out of the bathroom now; he noticed the back of her head where she sat on the couch watching one of her soaps. On the screen, an actress was passionately kissing a character Brian had never seen before, and Mama seemed rapt. She either didn't notice him or didn't bother to say anything. Brian didn't really care which, as long as she left him alone.

He didn't see Brandon with her, so he slipped upstairs as quietly as possible. A quick touch of his amulet wiped out the creak in the seventh step just as his foot touched it, and a second one swept the dust all clean. Those were things nobody would notice, or if they did then Brian could always say he'd fixed them by hand. Caution, caution was the thing to remember.

He didn't start to worry until he got to the bedroom and found no Brandon there either, and when a quick look in the upstairs bathroom and out the back window also failed to turn him up, Brian reluctantly decided he had no choice but to ask Mama, although he dreaded it.

He almost skipped the seventh step on his way down before remembering that he didn't have to anymore, and then he deliberately set his whole weight on it just to listen to the silence. He was starting to feel a little better about things. He might have to be careful, but his power was far from useless! He fixed two of the worst cracks in the wallpaper and removed a scratch on the banister without missing a beat, and then slipped through the kitchen as quiet as a whisper to stand hesitating at the entrance to the living room. Then he waited carefully for a commercial break before clearing his throat.

Mama didn't look back at him.

"What?" she asked irritably.

"Um, I just wondered if you knew where Brandon might be, Mama," he asked, in the humblest and most respectful voice he possessed. Mama hated disrespect above all other crimes.

"I don't know where he went. Go find him yourself if you want him," she said, in a tone that meant the subject was closed. Brian mumbled something that might have sounded like a thank-you, and then quickly retreated.

He searched rapidly through the house, checking all the places he could think of that were big enough for Brandon to be hiding in. He went back upstairs, looking in the hall closet and even venturing into Mama's room. No Brandon anywhere.

Then he thought of the attic. It seemed unlikely; Bran didn't usually go up there by himself, but there was always a first time for everything.

Brian quickly climbed up the narrow steps and poked his head through the door. It was too dark to see much, so he grabbed a rafter in one hand and felt his way forward, groping for the lamp stand. He couldn't remember switching it off earlier, but he guessed he must have.

When his eyes had adjusted to the darkness a bit, he immediately saw the lamp knocked over on the floor and the bulb smashed into a thousand pieces. He doubted Mama had been up there, so it must have been Brandon who'd done it.

"Great," he muttered.

He explored the boxes and piles of junk one at a time, being careful not to step on broken glass, and finally he found Brandon curled up in a ball in one corner, almost hidden behind a stack of old newspapers. Brian could barely see him at all except when he moved, and he seemed to be making no effort to come out. Then he realized the kid probably couldn't tell who he was in the dark.

"It's me, Beebo. Come out and tell me what's wrong," he said.

That got results. Brian staggered and barely kept from falling backwards into a mountain of rusty gas pipes heaped up behind him, almost bowled over by what felt like a human cannonball. Brandon wouldn't do anything but cry for a long time, and Brian soon gave up trying to ask him anything. It could wait.

Instead, he sat down and held him till he stopped crying before trying to talk to him again. Brandon still wasn't having any of that just yet, though, and the tears threatened to start all over again.

Eventually he calmed down to the point that Brian was able to pick him up and carry him out of the attic, and that was progress at least. It wasn't until they came out into the hall that he saw Brandon's left eye was almost swollen shut.

Brian went cold inside. Black eyes don't come from falling; only fists can do that.

Still, he said nothing, and took Brandon to their room. When he got there, he shut the door and sat down in his old rocking chair by the window. He knew, in a way, that this was just as much his fault as it was Mama's, because he was the one who'd wanted to go off and leave Brandon alone with her. He knew better. He couldn't pretend he didn't.

"Let me look at your eye, Beebo," he whispered. Brandon turned his head, looking up at him with one bright blue eye the exact same color as Brian's own. He couldn't see out of the other one, which gave him a strange, lopsided look.

Brian didn't care about being secret anymore. He closed his eyes, and imagined Brandon's eye the way it was supposed to be, and then kissed it. And when he looked again, there was no trace of the black eye left. Brandon looked at him soberly and laid his head on his brother's shoulder, and then it was Brian's turn to cry.

Unclouded Day

Is available now from your favorite retailer.

Free Sample of

Nightfall

Book One of the Tyke McGrath Series

Chapter One
Friday, April 25, 2036

At the worst possible moment, the power died.

The lab instantly went pitch dark, causing the tip of Micah McGrath's screwdriver to slip just the tiniest bit. Metal touched metal, and before he knew it one of the capacitors had discharged its built-up load right into the circuit board he'd been trying to fix.

Mike cursed and slammed his fist on the table in sheer frustration; what *else* could go wrong today? He didn't have *time* for things like this; he was supposed to have his dissertation finished in only three more weeks.

After a few seconds the university's emergency generator kicked in and the lights flickered back on. Then Mike promptly forgot about power glitches and burnt-out circuit boards, and his eyes widened in shocked surprise.

The tachometer was gone.

Mike knitted his brows and stared at the empty spot where the machine had been sitting just a few seconds ago. He rubbed his eyes to make sure he wasn't seeing things, but there was no doubt about it. The thing had definitely vanished.

He didn't know quite what to think about this unexpected development; in spite of all his efforts to fix it, the tachometer hadn't actually worked in years. And even if it had, he'd certainly never switched it on or set the controls for it to do anything. There was no reason he could think of why it shouldn't still be sitting there on the workbench.

His first thought was to wonder if the discharge from the capacitor might have inadvertently activated some obscure function, even though that seemed highly unlikely. Anytime the tachometer was operational it was always surrounded by a silvery bubble of energy several feet across, and he certainly would have noticed if anything like *that* had appeared.

But then again, Mike would have been the first to admit that he didn't really understand the blasted thing very well.

The machine was designed to capture and manipulate tachyons; those ghostly, faster-than-light particles which supposedly contained the power to foresee the future before it happened, and perhaps even to travel there.

True, Mike had never actually witnessed any of those things personally, but he'd heard plenty of stories from people who had. It was a fascinating subject, and when the time came to pick a research topic for his dissertation, there'd never been the slightest doubt that he'd choose to study tachyons. Never mind the fact that not everybody even believed they existed; Mike was determined to be the one who finally proved it to the world.

Dr. Bevels had smiled and called it "a learning experience", but that was okay; Mike was confident he'd show them all someday. He might only be twenty-three years old, but then again some of the greatest Nobel Prize winners in history had been in their early twenties. Mike himself was on track to become the youngest Ph.D. graduate in the history of the university, and surely that had to say *something* good about his prospects, didn't it?

He would never have admitted to harboring such grandiose thoughts, of course, but they were awfully nice to think about now and then.

He glanced at the clock and saw that it was already 4:15; close enough to call it a day if he liked. He normally stayed in the lab at least till five, but the inexplicable disappearance of the tachometer was a mystery he felt too mentally tired to tackle at the end of such a long day. Not to mention the fact that he'd skipped lunch and his stomach was beginning to suggest pretty urgently that it was high time to get something to eat. Maybe he could come back in the morning with a fresh mind and think of some new ideas.

He shut down his laptop and turned off the lights before locking the door and putting the keys in his pocket. When everything was in order, he tiredly climbed the stairs from the basement and walked outside to where his Jeep was parked in front of the athletics building. The science center and several other structures on campus were closed for renovations at the moment, which meant Mike had been assigned this little niche in the gym instead. It was adequate, perhaps, but certainly not very glamorous.

His "lab" had actually been somebody's office before Mike moved in, but he'd done his best to make it work as a research space, shoving the desk up against one wall and moving in a lab bench from the science building. He'd even hung a portrait of Tycho Brahe above the desk, the father of modern astronomy and one of his particular heroes. Heaven knows he needed some inspiration and encouragement now and then.

There were more people than usual gathered in scattered groups outside, but Mike was too preoccupied with his own thoughts to pay much attention to that. He fired up the Jeep, intending to drive home, find something to eat, and then do absolutely nothing for the rest of the evening.

He heard police sirens wailing somewhere off to the north, and wondered idly what was going on. He supposed he'd hear about it soon enough, if it mattered.

He drove slowly down the quiet street next to the university, and other than the traffic lights not working there didn't seem to be anything out of the ordinary. Just a typical springtime afternoon. An old lady weeding her azaleas waved at him, and he smiled and waved back. He passed the fire station and the white-columned library, then the bank and his favorite coffee shop and the big red-brick Victorian courthouse on the town square. Almost home!

The house he shared with his best friend Joey Wilder was built on the side of a hill maybe half a block past the courthouse, where Third Street ran steeply down to cross the railroad tracks. But then as Mike swung into the front yard, he noticed an anomaly. There was a small crowd of people standing in front of the church across the street, but it was what they were staring at that immediately caught his attention and left him every bit as speechless as they were.

Just past the church, the street ended. Where it had once swept on down the hill to the tracks, now it just. . . stopped. And where the street used to be, now there were only trees. Large ones, that looked as if they'd been there since the day the world began.

That was shocking enough, but when Mike raised his eyes swiftly to look out over the treetops, he was in for an even greater shock. Where there had once been railroad tracks and factories and houses scattered thickly as far as he could see across the valley, now there was nothing. No tracks, no houses, no streets. Just an unbroken canopy of green that stretched all the way to the horizon.

Mike broke his stupefaction and walked slowly the last hundred feet or so to the end of the pavement, reaching out to touch the trunk of a massive oak tree that stood right in the middle of where the street should have been. The bark was rough and solid. Then he knelt down and touched the edge of the pavement, and found that it cut off as sharply as if someone had sliced it with a gigantic razor blade and left only this side behind.

The cut extended smoothly in both directions from where he knelt. To the east, it crossed the parking lot between the church and where the Family Life Center should have been, and then it passed quickly behind the church itself and out of Mike's sight. In the other direction it passed right through his own back yard, almost clipping off the corner of his house as a matter of fact. He could see a little bit farther in that direction, and it seemed that the razor's edge had a slight curve to it, though it was hard to be sure.

A dark suspicion flirted at the edge of his mind, but he dismissed the thought immediately. It *couldn't* be.

He gingerly took a step past the end of the street, and then another. Soon he was standing amongst an almost silent forest of trees that whispered tranquilly in the breeze. They were unusually large and thick, but otherwise no different than any other trees he'd ever seen.

Except for the fact that they hadn't been there when he left the house that morning, of course. The trunks were widely spaced and the forest floor was level enough to drive a small car through, if the driver were careful.

After a few seconds he quit gaping at the trees and walked swiftly back up the hill to his own front door. As soon as he got inside the house, he found Joey fiddling with the little battery-powered radio they kept for emergencies.

"Where have you been, Mike? Have you seen what's going on out there?" Joey asked. He was almost exactly two years older than Mike himself, but they'd known each other ever since Mike could remember.

"Yeah, I see it. I don't believe it, but I definitely see it. Have you heard anything on the radio?" Mike asked.

"No, I couldn't find any batteries for it. All the ones I've tried are already dead," Joey said. For some reason Mike had never been able to force himself to throw away old batteries, and as a result almost every shelf and drawer in the house contained at least a few of them. Joey had complained about it times without number.

"I guess I better run go get some, then. I'll be back in a little while. One of us better stay here and keep an eye on the house, though, don't you think?" he asked, and Joey shrugged.

He grabbed a chocolate chip granola bar from the kitchen before running back outside to where the Jeep was parked. He usually walked or rode his bike around town, partly to save gas and partly to get some exercise, but at the moment he cared more about speed than anything else.

He didn't head directly for the store, though. As soon as he was out on the street, he began following the razor-edge to the west. There were places where it had sliced right through the middle of houses or buildings, with the other half disappearing like magic, with no trace of rubble or destruction. Except in a few cases, where the remainder of the structure had collapsed from the stress and fallen into the trees that crowded right up to the line. After a while, he also noted that the tree branches were cut off in a similar fashion; not even so much as a twig crossed the boundary.

People were gathered all along his route, staring at the trees with attitudes that ranged anywhere from mild curiosity to dumbfounded amazement. No one seemed panicky or hysterical, and some were even laughing and socializing, as if the whole thing were some kind of huge joke.

The line crossed right behind the National Guard armory and the post office, cut through some more houses and streets, then clipped the corner of the old cemetery. Then Mike saw some major damage; the blue jean factory and the junior high school had been sliced in half, and both of them had mostly collapsed. Thank God school had already been over for the day.

The line continued on into another residential area where Mike couldn't follow, but he drove quickly to Pine Street and picked it up again. It ran right through the middle of the Arby's drive-thru, and then plunged back (again) into residential areas.

Mike doggedly followed the line as far as he could. It ran right behind the university football stadium, and sliced off the main highway out of town exactly where Pizza Hut should have been. That was a bad scene; someone in a black Lexus had smashed into the trees when the highway disappeared in front of her, and two other cars had piled up behind the first one. There was no ambulance to be seen; nothing but the smashed Lexus, and three bewildered-looking cops who kept glancing at the trees.

Mike made an illegal U-turn and drove urgently back to his lab, parking the Jeep right by the front door. The group of students from earlier had disappeared, which suited him just as well. The fewer witnesses there were, the better.

As soon as he got inside the gym he heard the sound of someone playing basketball, apparently unaware of what was going on.   He rushed downstairs to his little cubbyhole and unlocked the door, almost stubbing his toe in his haste to get inside.   There was a city map in his desk drawer, and he quickly unfolded it on the workbench next to where the tachometer had been.   Then he took a pencil and carefully marked every location where he'd seen the razor cut pass.

He noticed immediately that it was an almost perfect circle, and with shaking hands he drew three separate diameter lines with a ruler so as to find the center point.

The lines met right where his lab stood.

A cold knot of fear threatened to cut off his breath when he saw that, because there could be only one explanation for everything he'd seen.   Namely, the tachometer must have been activated somehow by the discharge of the capacitor, and then dragged the entire central core of Arkadelphia to some unknown point in the future.

Never mind that it hadn't been switched on, or that an ocean of trees looked nothing like any kind of future Mike had ever anticipated, or that he'd never imagined the tachometer could swallow an area big enough to engulf nearly a whole town. Those were incidentals which could be explained later.   In the meantime, there wasn't a shred of doubt in his mind about what had actually happened.

You've really done it now, boy, he thought to himself.

Even worse, he knew it wouldn't be long before other people started connecting the dots and reaching similar conclusions. Oh, they might not know exactly what happened, true, but it wouldn't take a genius to figure out who was responsible for it, as soon as somebody noticed whose lab was at the exact center of the circle. His research wasn't a secret, and neither was the location of his lab.   One of the few things he liked about working in the gym instead of in the science building was the extra peace and privacy, but that wouldn't mean a thing once the whole town was looking for him.   And he was sure they soon would be.

He quickly gathered up his own research notes along with Dr. Garza's original lab manuals. He didn't dare leave anything at the lab to be confiscated or destroyed, and least of all *those.* He even took the laptop, although he felt guilty about that. It technically belonged to the university, not to him, and he wasn't actually supposed to leave campus with it. He was careful to make sure no one saw him removing items from the building, since that would only focus attention on him that much faster.

He finished loading up and calmly drove away, thinking hard. Most people in town probably didn't really comprehend what had happened yet, and some of them might not even know. Things still seemed bizarrely normal at the moment. But Mike could guess what was coming within the next few weeks, if a world of trees were really all there was in this future time. Food and clean water would run out quickly, and when that happened, it was only a matter of time until cholera or dysentery reared its ugly head. And with no medicine to speak of. . . He shuddered.

Without wasting another second, he drove immediately to the bank. The lobby was already closed, of course, but the drive through was still open. He pulled up to the window and stopped, breathing a sigh of relief when he saw the girl at the computer. It was Allison, and he knew her well enough that she might do him a favor. He smiled and waved at her so she could see his face, and she smiled back when she recognized him. He pushed the call button and noted with satisfaction that the bank must have had a generator, since the machine was still working. Thank God for small blessings.

Mike quickly wrote a check for 2419.85, which was every nickel he had in his account.

Allison took the check and sent the cash and his driver's license back out, which he took with trembling hands. Somehow he managed to smile again and thank Allison before he left. He stuffed the cash in his pocket and then drove directly to the grocery store. If trouble were coming then he wasn't taking any chances.

It was busier than it should have been at that time of day, which worried him; apparently word was getting around and people were starting to get uneasy. The bread and milk sections were practically wiped out already, he noticed, but those weren't the kinds of things Mike had in mind anyway.

He grabbed a shopping cart and filled it as quickly as he could with anything that wouldn't spoil, especially canned goods. Then he filled two more. Not just with food, either; he quickly cleaned out everything useful he could find in the pharmacy section, too, including all the antibiotics and bandages, all the painkillers, and all the major vitamins. As an afterthought, he grabbed two handfuls of lighters, six bottles of chlorine bleach, and anything else he could think of that was useful and couldn't be replaced. The checkout lady gave him an amused look when he got to the cash register.

"You think the end of the world is comin', honey?" she asked with a chuckle.

"No, ma'am, just making sure," he said. That only made her laugh again, as he hoped it would. It took a while to pay for everything and get it loaded in the back of the Jeep, but there was still one more stop to make before he dared go home. His usual sporting goods store was gone, but there was a hole-in-the-wall gun shop downtown, and as soon as he got there Mike bought every .22 bullet they had. He got some raised eyebrows for that, but he couldn't have cared less.

He didn't park in the front yard when he got home as he usually would have. Instead, he backed into the garage to unload his supplies.

"Where have you *been,* dude? Don't you know-" Joey began, coming out of the kitchen door into the garage. Then he saw the mountain of grocery bags and trailed off.

"Uh, do you know something you're not telling me?" he finally asked.

"I'm not sure. Help me carry all this stuff inside and then we'll talk about it and try to figure things out. But first let's lock all the doors, and the windows too for that matter," Mike added as an afterthought.

"Whatever you say, buddy," Joey said, with a shrug that indicated he clearly believed Mike had lost his mind.

They quickly locked every door and window, even drawing the blinds and drapes. Joey was mostly quiet during all this, even when Mike started taking food down to the basement instead of the kitchen, but when he saw the case of bullets that must have been too much for him to keep silent about.

"Hold on a minute, dude. Seriously, what's going on? If you're gonna come home and start acting like it's world war three you should at least tell me what's up," he said.

"You're absolutely right, but let's finish putting this stuff away first. As soon as that's done I'll tell you everything, I promise," Mike said. Joey looked like he wanted to argue about it some more, but then seemed to change his mind.

"All right, then," he finally said. And he was as good as his word; he worked as fast as Mike did to get all the groceries hauled down to the basement and hidden carefully behind the old furnace. Not just the food and supplies, either, but Mike's computer and lab notes, also. Only when everything was safely stashed away did they both sit down at the kitchen table and partially relax.

Nightfall

Is available now from your favorite retailer.

Author's Note

Truesilver wasn't originally planned. But I received so many requests to hear more about Zach Trewick and his adventures, I wanted to give the fans what they asked for. So in a way this book is every bit as much the creation of my readers as it is mine.

There was always the possibility of dealing with the woken-up wolves, of course, and that's the path I chose to take in this book. I did my usual thing and ran down whatever rabbit holes appealed to me at the time, since I've always thought writing should be at least as much fun as reading.

Certain readers with a sharp eye for details will probably have noticed that the mountains north of Langley are the Ouachitas, and therefore not technically part of the Ozarks. But since in the wider world they usually do get lumped together under the same name, I didn't see any harm in following that general rule. One need not be pedantic about such things.

That said, most of the things in the book are real-life people and places. Juan de Velasco really existed, his ship was really the *San Andrés,* and he really sank in a storm off Mexico in 1600. The Skullcrusher Mountains are real, and so were Madryn of Gwent and Tristan of Tintagel, whose sword was really named Mercy and which has really belonged to all the Kings of England since Edward the Confessor. Iridium is a real metal, with the same properties which I described in the book, and along with platinum it has occasionally been called truesilver. They do indeed make spark plugs and fountain pens from it. Cape Mendocino is similar to what I described, including the exact location and depth of the very underwater canyon Zach and the others visited, which is called (uninterestingly) Mendocino Canyon.

Doing research on obscure topics like octopus wrestling or the history of sword fighting is actually one of the biggest pleasures of coming up with these adventures. I have a legitimate reason to satisfy my curiosity about everything under the sun, and what's not to love about that?

This book contains characters which appear in other books not directly related to *The Last Werewolf Hunter* series. I've always liked big, intricately connected worlds in which I can learn more about any character I like just by finding another book. It's a closer reflection of the real world, and it adds so much more depth and richness to all the stories. The story of Cameron and Joan continues in *Tycho,* for example.

Cody McGrath's tale is told in *Many Waters (Book Two of the Stones of Song Series),* a book which is closely related to this series even though it's not really part of it. But since Zach found the story of Cody's fight with Layla Garza so interesting (even though he never asked about it), I thought other readers might be curious, too. Matthieu Doucet plays a big part in that story, and so does Brandon Stone, from *Unclouded Day.* The tales of the five Curse-Breakers often cross paths in unusual and unexpected ways.

But in the meantime, I hope my readers enjoy this fourth book of Zach's adventures as much as they have his past ones. In the future, as Zach himself says, he'll move on to greater things; to fighting whatever kinds of evils there may be in the world, so you never really know what might pop up in the future. This time it was evil sorcerers, tomorrow it could be anything. I think that's a broad enough scope to provide Zach with adventure and purpose for the rest of his life.

William Woodall
June 20, 2013

Discussion Questions

1. Zach warns Cameron not to let himself get too close to Joan. Considering how things turned out, do you think that was good advice or not? Explain why you think so.

2. Joan was very untrusting and defiant when she first woke up. Why do you think she might have felt that way? What kind of experiences might she have had that led her to become the type of person she was?

3. Matthieu tells Zach that he has a likable aura which encourages people to help him. Have you ever known people whose personalities made you instantly like them (or dislike them), even before you really knew them? Talk about some of those experiences.

4. Zach says that all tormenters have suck-ups and toadies, and that these people are just as black-hearted and evil as the ones they look up to. How do you feel about this? Do you agree with that assessment, or do you think ringleaders are worse than their followers to some extent? Explain why you think as you do.

5. At one point, Zach quotes the ancient proverb *Death Before Dishonor,* with the meaning that one should never betray the principles he/she believes in, no matter how high the cost. Discuss how you feel about this concept of honor. Are there ever any circumstances when exceptions should be made? Explain your thoughts.

6. Zach says that since God is outside of time, then so are our prayers to Him, and therefore it's possible for us to be the partial cause of things which took place long before we were born, provided we don't already know what the outcome was. Discuss this idea. Are there any people or events in the past that you would want to pray for? Share some of these things and why you'd want to pray for them.

7. What do you think Zach meant when he said that not all the monsters in the world are cursed ones? Explain what you think he meant by this and the ways it might apply in everyday life.

8. Zach says that love is a beautiful thing, and the whole world bows down in awe at the sight of it. Do you think this is true? Are there any exceptions?

9. According to the book, there's a huge difference between magic and miracles; namely, that magic is the power to do as we please, while miracles must be asked for and may or may not be granted. Discuss this difference and why it matters.

10. The "theme" of a story is the underlying message or messages about life the author is trying to convey. It is the lesson or moral of the story, such as "Love conquers all". What do you think the theme of *Truesilver* is? (There can be more than one.)

11. Zach says that when you start thinking about leaving behind a place that you love, then you have a tendency to pull it close to your heart while you still can. Discuss this. Do you think this is true? What are some ways you think the area where you live has affected who you are and how you see the world?

12. Zach and Cameron have been very close for a long time and have a strong bond. How do you think Cameron felt, when he saw himself in the future and knew there was no coming back? Describe any mixed feelings you think he might have had and why.

13. Cameron named his first son Christopher, which Zach's parents had once intended to be *his* name. What do you think Cameron's purposes for doing this might have been? (There can be several.)

14. Near the end, Zach says he wishes he knew more about Cody McGrath's story, but he doesn't actually ask. Have there ever been times in a story when you were left wondering about what happened to a certain character or how a certain sequence of events turned out? Do you prefer to have everything tied up at the end, or would you rather have some things left unanswered?

15. What are some of the mistakes you think the characters in this book made, and what should they have done differently?

The Curse-Breaker Books
By William Woodall

Long ago, there was a Godly woman named Marybeth Trewick, who for various reasons found herself married to a rich but wicked man named Daniel who practiced all kinds of evil. She could only watch helplessly as her five sons grew up to become just as wicked as their father, and as her only daughter was forced to flee for her life lest she be killed.

But in the midst of her despair, God sent Marybeth a dream that after seven generations had passed, there would be five boys born to replace and redeem the ones that she had lost. These five would be breakers of curses and fighters against all things wicked and evil, and each of them would have the same vividly blue eyes, the same color as Marybeth's.

And even though the Curse-Breakers are each called to very different tasks in the world, the basic goal of fighting evil and loving God is always the same. These are their names and stories.

Brian Stone: The oldest curse-breaker, Brian's task is to save his brother's life and to remind men of Heaven by showing them the beauty of what could have been if the world had never fallen.

Cody McGrath: Two years younger than Brian, Cody is called to break the power of a dangerous sorceress. He's a dreamer of true dreams and a healer of the lost and broken-hearted.

Zachary Trewick: Four years younger than Cody, Zach is called to destroy one of the worst remaining aspects of his ancestor's wickedness; the werewolf curse which most of his family still embrace wholeheartedly.

Cameron Parker: Cameron and Zach are the same age, not to mention third cousins and best friends. Cameron has a big role to play in the struggle against the wolves, and later becomes the leader of all the survivors of Earth.

Brandon Stone: Brian's little brother, Brandon is three years younger than Cameron and Zach. He has a gift to know the meaning of dreams, and he is called to defend the weak and to uphold all that is righteous and true.

The Curse-Breaker Books form a collection of related stories about these five boys and sometimes their children. Each series tells the tale of a different Curse-Breaker (or sometimes more than one), but they also fit together in ways you wouldn't expect, in order to form a single unified storyline. It's helpful to read the books in order if possible, but it's not strictly necessary. You can read more about each series on the following pages.

The Last Werewolf Hunter Series
By William Woodall

Zach Trewick always thought he'd become a writer someday, or maybe play baseball for the Texas Rangers. What he never imagined in his craziest dreams was that he'd find himself dodging bullets and crashing cars off mountainsides, let alone that he'd ever be expected to break the ancient werewolf curse which hangs over his family.

But Zach is the last of the werewolf hunters, the long-foretold Curse-Breaker who can wipe out the wolves forever, and he's not the type to give up just because of a few minor setbacks. . .

Cry for the Moon: What would you do, if your family wanted you to become a monster? What if they wouldn't take no for an answer? When 12 year old Zach faces questions like these, he seems to have only one choice; *run*. Thus begins a long search for refuge, and perhaps redemption also.

Behind Blue Eyes: When a stranger kidnaps him from his own back yard, Zach soon finds that the past isn't quite as dead as he might wish. For the time has come at last for Zach and his cousin Cameron to break the wolf curse forever; and his family has no intention of letting that happen.

More Golden Than Day: When his girlfriend Jolie and then Cameron fall into the hands of the wolves, Zach has no choice but to take on his enemies for a second round. Only this time the stakes are horribly high, and if he fails he may end up losing everything he's ever loved.

Truesilver: When a family of wicked ex-wolves is accidentally awakened, Zach soon finds himself locked in a desperate fight for survival that he never anticipated. And even though he's sworn an oath to fight evil to the utmost of his power, there are times when courage is awfully hard to come by.

* * * * * * *

"If you are looking for a story about a boy who learns valuable lessons about family, love, friendship and God this is the book for you. I recommend this book to a pre-teen or adult. I truly enjoyed this book."
-Rae, *My Book Addiction Reviews*

"I found myself captivated with the story and could not stop reading until I reached the final page. Everything about this story is thought-provoking. Readers of all ages will appreciate this wonderfully told story,"
-Jancy, Kansas

The Stones of Song Series
By William Woodall

"There's a thing called magnanimity, or greatness of heart, and to me it's the most beautiful thing that ever there was. It means courage, but it's more than that. It means to cast aside all thought of yourself for the sake of another, like Moses in Gilead or the martyrs who died with a smile on their face. In its own small way it's a reflection of the Lord Jesus at Calvary, and therefore of God, the Light so beautiful that no one who sees it can ever turn away."

So says Cody McGrath, and in many ways that statement is the central theme of this series; the casting away of self for love of another, the scorning of selfishness in all its forms.

These are the stories of the Stone family: Brian, Jenny, Lisa, and Brandon, and some of the people they know and love, most notably Cody. All of them were called for great and glorious things, though sometimes only after great suffering and many mistakes.

Unclouded Day: Brian Stone's life isn't easy. Abandoned by his father, abused by his alcoholic mother, and mocked by his classmates, his only treasures are his beloved little brother and his old guitar. This is the tale of his journey to find the Fountain of Youth, and perhaps to save the world.

Many Waters: Lisa Stone is a small-town waitress with heavy burdens to bear. Cody is a young cowboy with mystical dreams and some very dangerous enemies. But when the two of them must face down an evil witch who tries to destroy their very lives, it seems only a miracle can save them.

Bran the Blessed: Brandon Stone hasn't always made the right choices in life, but he's never found himself in quite such deep trouble as this. But even though his life seems ruined forever, Bran still has a high calling to answer. . . if he can find the courage.

* * * * * * *

"I would absolutely, without reservation, encourage you to read this wonderful novel, even if you aren't the fantasy genre type. It was a blessing."
-Sue, Reflections and Reviews

"There are so many nuggets of truth in this book. It's about Heaven. It's about bad things happening for a reason. It's about deciding for yourself what truly matters most in life. It's a really good book!"
-Tattie, Christian Fiction Ebooks

The Tyke McGrath Series
By *William Woodall*

In the year 2154, the world has become a dangerous place. Extremist groups would like nothing better than to wipe out humanity completely, and even the people sworn to defend civilization against such threats have become deeply corrupt and untrustworthy.

When a virulent plague destroys all warm-blooded life on Earth, a small band of survivors clings to life on the partially-terraformed Moon. But fresh dangers lie in wait for the unwary; nor have they left behind all the wickedness in the hearts of men.

Nightfall: When Micah McGrath suddenly finds himself thrust into a dangerous and ugly future after a lab accident, his only choice is to make the best life for himself that he can. But when the secret police get wind of his research into time travel, he soon finds himself in deep trouble indeed.

Tycho: Tycho McGrath is a high school honor student in Florida when he discovers a terrifying secret: a man-made bacterium is about to wipe out all warm-blooded life on Earth within days. The only hope for survival is to flee at once, a plan which carries its own set of unexpected dangers.

Avenger: After spotting an SOS coming from the abandoned Moon, the survivors must organize a rescue mission. But the expedition quickly becomes far more complicated, leading them to the icy world of Titan in search of a holy mountain that no human eye has ever seen.

Freedom: When a cruel and power-hungry military commander on Venus decides to reconquer Earth, the only thing he needs is the formula for Tyke's Orion vaccine. The survivors soon find themselves locked into a bitter battle over the future of mankind, and who will inherit the Earth after all.

Elysium: What began as a simple mission to recover lost comrades in the Martian desert quickly turns deadly when Tyke and the others find *themselves* stranded on the Red Planet, with only the slimmest of chances to make it home again, or to fulfill the destiny which God has in store for them.

* * * * * * *

"Reminiscent of Freedom's Landing, by Anne McCaffrey, Tycho combines the best of traditional space-exploration sci-fi with modern apocalyptic fiction. For any fans of hard science fiction, it doesn't get much better than this." **- Liz, OH2 Reviews**

"This story was awesome! A must-read book if you like sci-fi." *-Scott, Georgia*

<u>Trewick Family Tree</u>

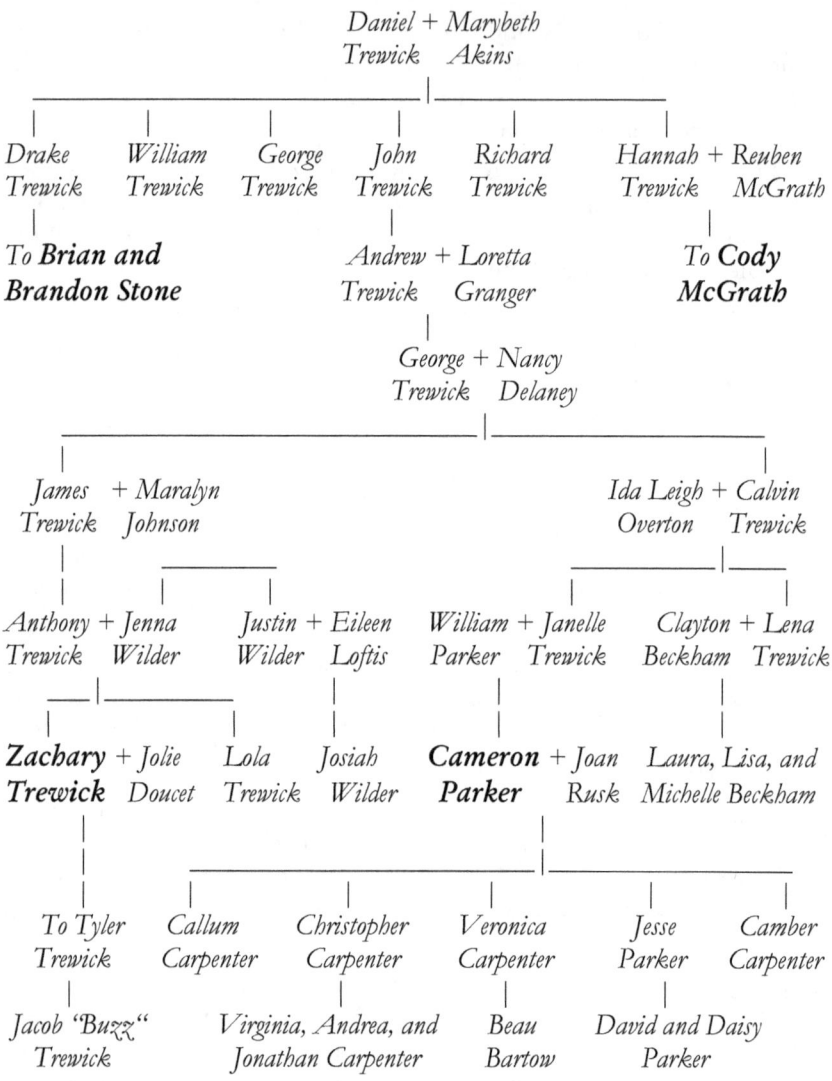

1. Curse-Breakers are in bold.
2. Cameron Parker later changed his name to Philip Carpenter.
3. Tyler Trewick is Zach's great-grandson.
4. Lisa Beckham's husband is Logan Tygart.
5. Laura Beckham's husband is Heath Coates, son of Albert Coates.

Trewick Family Tree

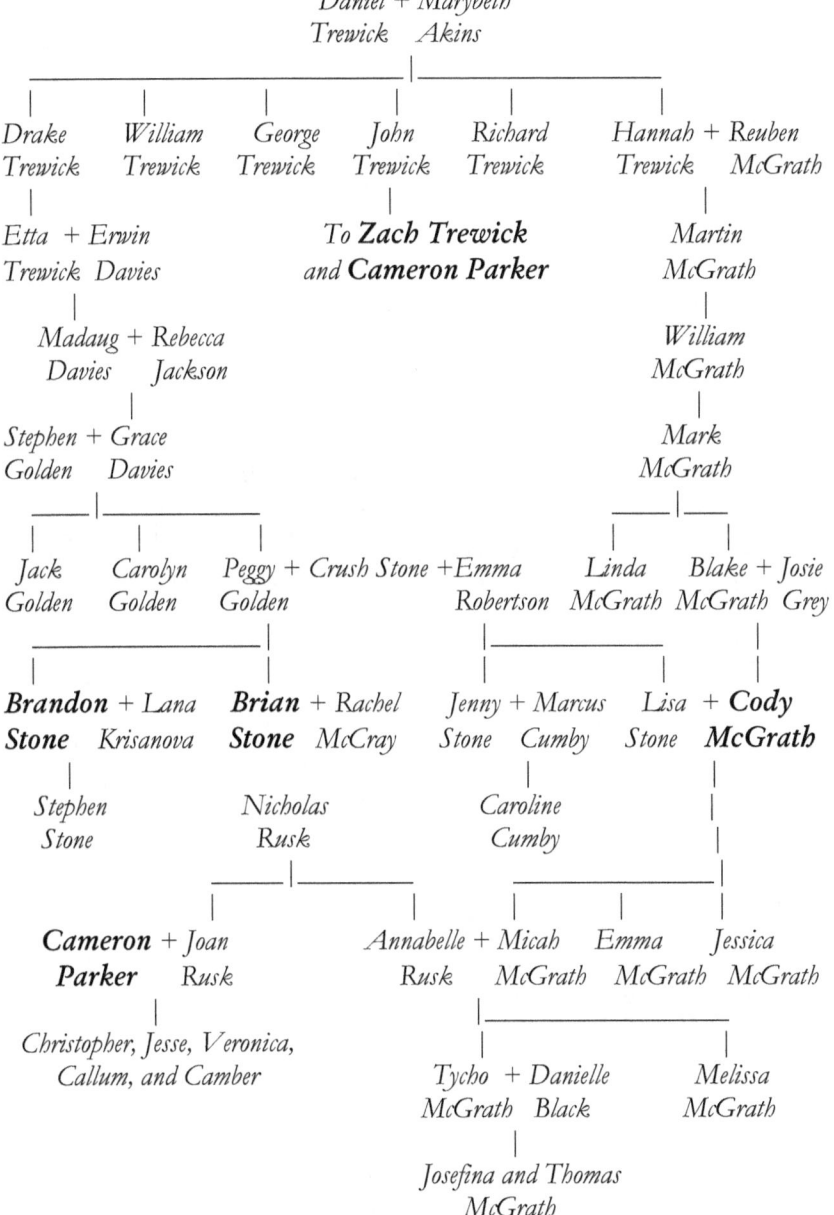

Doucet Family Tree

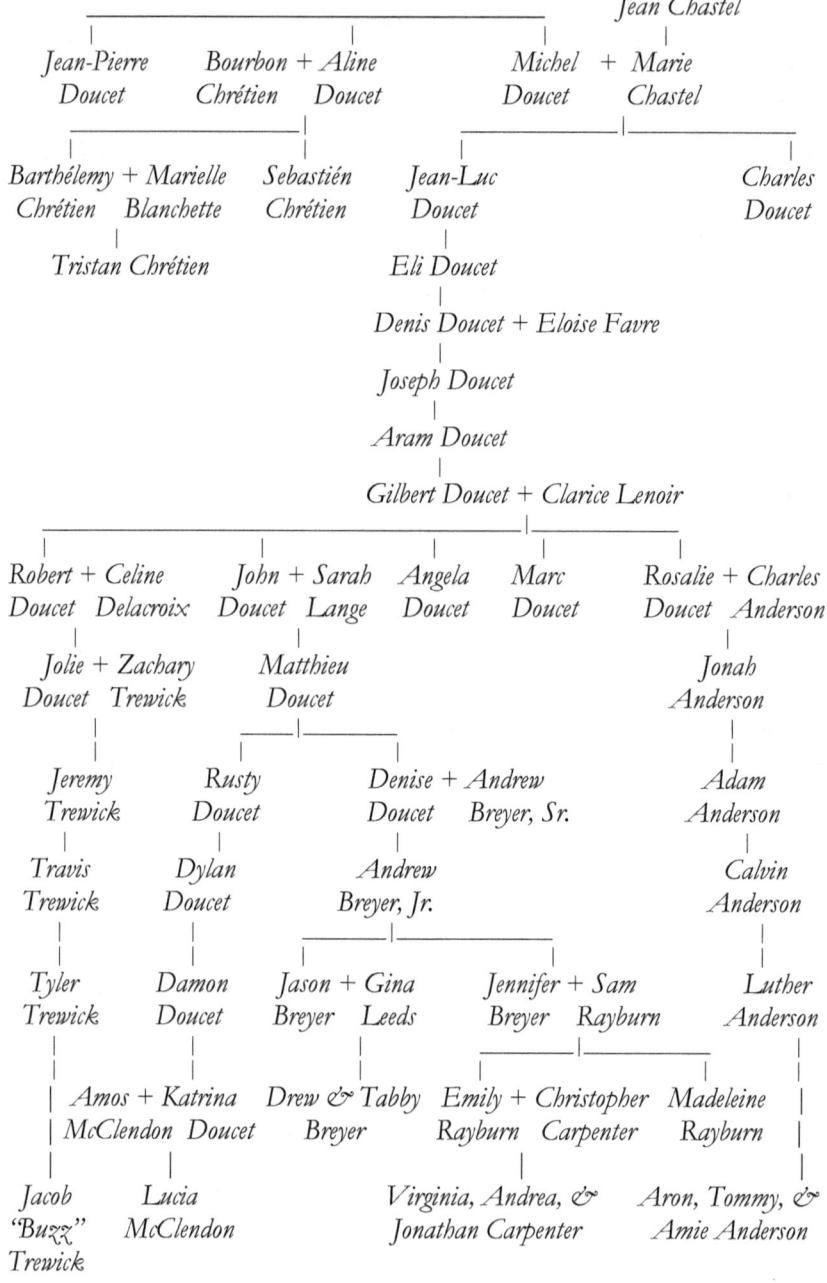

Bartow Family Tree

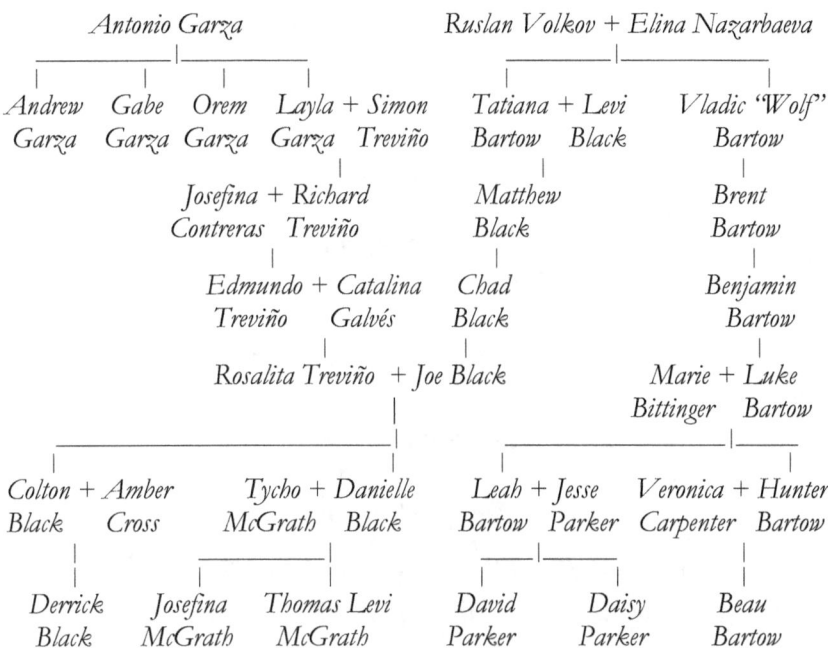

Jones and Golden Family Trees

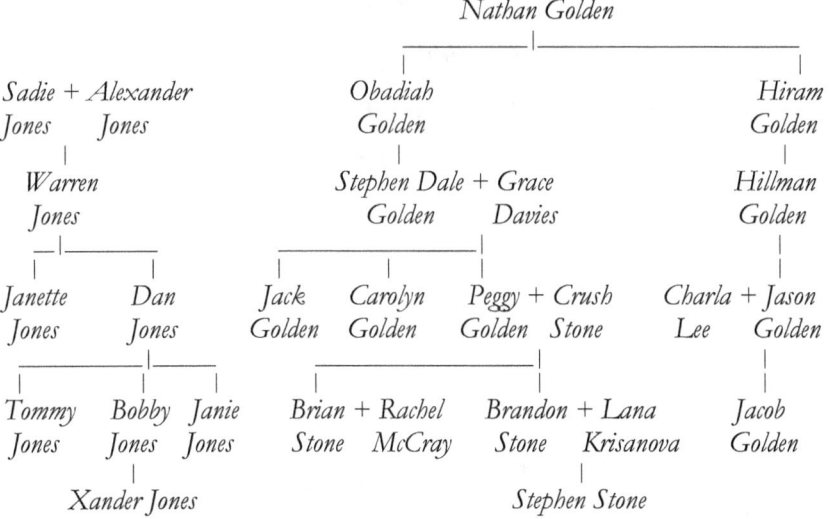

*If you'd like to find out more about
these and other books,
please visit:*

*William Woodall's
Official Author Website*

www.williamwoodall.org

Here you will find:

Free short stories

Discussion questions for teachers and book clubs

Free sample chapters of all my books

Photos of characters and locations for each story

Articles

Interviews

Quotable Quotes

Contact Information

And much, much more!